# MAGIC UNCORKED

ANNABEL CHASE

Storm

Ebook ISBN: 978-1-83700-197-2
Paperback ISBN: 978-1-83700-198-9

Cover design: Alexandra Allden
Cover images: Shutterstock

Published by Storm Publishing.
For further information, visit:
www.stormpublishing.co

# ONE

Hercules rescued Libbie Stark from a nightmare that involved her car careening off a cliff. She wasn't sure why she bothered to set the alarm when the Irish Setter nudged her awake every morning at seven. Never mind that the dog could easily make his desire for the great outdoors known to Chris, who was undoubtedly already downstairs with a hot cup of coffee and a bowl of cereal. Libbie knew her boyfriend would've gladly slept until noon each day in the summer if his body clock would allow it. As a P.E. teacher at the local high school, though, he was too accustomed to early rising.

Libbie peeled off the covers and reluctantly left the comfort of her cocoon. "Just don't pee on the carpet, I beg you."

Hercules had far too much exuberance for a ten-year-old dog, as far as she was concerned. She made her way down the staircase, careful not to trip. Even at his age, the dog had a habit of zipping in front of her on the steps when she least expected it.

She arrived in the kitchen to find Chris hunched over a plate of scrambled eggs. Not cereal today, then. She glanced at the pan still on the stovetop, knowing perfectly well she'd find it empty. She was the professional chef in the house, which somehow meant that Chris only cooked for himself and not for her.

"Hey, sunshine," she said when he failed to acknowledge her.

Chris grunted in response. He wasn't a morning person—not an issue for Libbie most of the year because he was out the door first, followed by her kids leaving for school. Weather permitting, she'd sit outside with a cup of coffee, Hercules at her feet, and listen to the birds chirping before she headed to work. If she were lucky, she'd spot a red cardinal, her favorite. Interesting that, in the animal kingdom, beauty tended to be the hallmark of males, unlike the human world where women were prized for their looks. One of the things Chris had told her when they'd first met was that he liked that she didn't try too hard like other women. Even now, Libbie wasn't entirely sure what he'd meant. She'd smiled and nodded, as though she understood, and he'd bought her a funnel cake at the carnival. She'd eaten it, dusting powdered sugar down the front of her dress.

Libbie opened the door to the backyard, and the dog bolted past her into the summer sunshine.

"You might want to watch him," Chris said. "There was another rabbit in your garden this morning."

Libbie peered outside at her neglected herb garden. She knew she had to make more time for it, but it seemed to slide further and further down the list of priorities. At least the rabbits were enjoying it.

She poured a cup of coffee and was relieved to see there was enough for a full cup. Small mercies.

"Your kids are still asleep," Chris said in an accusatory tone.

"I figured."

"You should probably wake them."

Libbie bit the inside of her cheek to keep from laughing. Her kids worked all summer long, whereas Chris spent the summer fishing and doing whatever he pleased. It would be fine if they weren't strapped for cash, but Chris was always on her about not wasting money to the point where Libbie worried they'd end up living paycheck-to-paycheck if they weren't careful. She didn't understand how money could've gotten so tight. She was a frugal shopper by nature, too afraid to spend unless there was a sale, and she'd been very conservative when she'd refinanced the mortgage after her divorce. Then again, two growing teenagers weren't cheap.

"It's Fourth of July weekend," she said. "Let them sleep. They'll be busy enough later."

Sixteen-year-old Josh worked as a lifeguard at the lake for Club Cloverleaf. The lake and pools would be packed this weekend with seasonal renters, as well as the locals out in full force. Thirteen-year-old Courtney would be complaining of a sore arm after scooping ice cream all afternoon at Cone Hut, her father's business. Libbie and Nick had divorced four years ago. Thankfully, the split had been amicable. Libbie avoided conflict as much as humanly possible; it made her too uncomfortable.

Chris slurped his coffee, a habit Libbie secretly hated. It reminded her of Josh when he was a little boy, sucking every drop of chocolate milk out of the carton. The comparison wasn't flattering.

She grabbed a banana muffin from the plastic container on the counter. She and Courtney had baked them two days ago, and they'd retained their fresh taste.

"Are you going around the lake before work?" Chris asked.

Libbie joined him at the table. "Just the short route. I want to get there a little early today and try to talk to Joe again about my ideas."

Libbie had been working up the nerve to broach the subject of menu changes with her boss for almost a year now. Business wasn't exactly booming, and Libbie knew from town gossip that the menu was part of the problem. Unfortunately, Joe Romano was set in his ways. He liked his menu to reflect his personal taste in food and nothing else, which would be fine if his tastes weren't so bland. Even the name of the restaurant was bland. Basecamp was for mountain climbers or astronauts, not foodies.

Chris sucked the remaining milk from the bowl. "If you're serious about losing weight, you need to do more than paddle around the lake in a kayak. You should think about what you're eating and drinking too. There's a lot of sugar in those cocktails of yours."

Libbie bristled at the jab. Chris disliked her Friday night cocktail club. He couldn't understand why she chose to spend one night a week with her girlfriends when she could be home on the couch with him, watching whatever show he deemed worthy of their time and attention. Libbie had been a member of the cocktail club long before Chris Pennington had come around, however, and she had no intention of leaving it.

"I'm sure you're right," she said, unwilling to argue. Arguing created tension, and tension made Libbie anxious. She shouldn't have mentioned the stubborn ten pounds she wanted to lose. Now he'd raise the topic at inopportune moments, like in the middle of a party or at a restaurant in front of the waiter. *Are you sure you want dessert?* he'd say, just as she was pointing to the chocolate mousse on the menu. Then he'd order a slice of pie for himself because, of course, he didn't need to contend with hormonal changes in middle age. At least not the kind that created a spare tire. Chris was in good shape and he knew it.

Libbie finished her muffin and coffee and let the dog in before hurrying upstairs to change. Kayaking during the summer months was a little tricky because Lake Cloverleaf was more crowded, even in the mornings. Libbie had to be mindful of boats and jet skis as she made her way along the perimeter of the clover-shaped lake.

She sauntered across the street and through the neighbor's yard to her kayak. Her house wasn't lakefront but the Seymours' was, and they'd been letting her use their property as a cut-through since she'd moved in fifteen years ago. Of course, she and Nick had been married then with a one-year-old, not that it mattered. June and Trent Seymour were the kind of neighbors everyone wanted and few were fortunate enough to have.

Libbie made her way past their blooming azaleas to the shaded spot where her kayak waited. The red paint was chipped in places, but it was in otherwise excellent condition, despite years of regular use. She hated when the weather changed and it became too cold to enjoy the lake. Kayaking was more than exercise for Libbie; it was her time to think without interruption. She used it the way other people used yoga, as a way to self-reflect and calm herself before facing the rest of her day. She dreaded the winter months when she was confined indoors most of the time.

Libbie settled into the kayak and tilted her head back, enjoying the warmth of the sun on her face. Thanks to her pale skin and freckles, she made sure her sunscreen had the maximum SPF. Her great-grandmother had lost her nose to skin cancer, something Libbie very much hoped to avoid.

As she paddled, she rehearsed her speech to Joe, saying the words out loud to hear how they sounded. Oftentimes, she lost her nerve when she needed to broach a difficult subject and suffered in silence, but she was determined to persevere today. Meatloaf and chicken parm were fine as staples, but it wouldn't kill him to draw in more customers with slightly edgier fare. At forty-eight years old, she'd grown tired of cooking the same dishes day in and day out. She was ready for a new challenge.

Libbie limited her circuit to one 'leaf' of the lake and cut across the middle to return to the Seymours' yard. She could tell from the number of boats already on the water that it was going to be a busy weekend.

As she crossed the road back to her house, she spotted her ex-husband in the driveway. Nick turned toward the sound of her feet crunching on the gravel.

"I should've known," he said, smiling. Nick was a nice guy when they'd married and was still a nice guy, even after the divorce. Their marriage, however, had been a mistake from the beginning, and the birth of their two children didn't change that fact. Libbie had been eager to create her own family as a means of escape from her situation, and Nick had been willing to take the plunge. They'd parted as friends, and he'd moved two streets over to make shared custody easier. Libbie wasn't the least bit surprised when he met and married a younger woman. Nick and Olivia had a toddler named Harry.

Nick gestured to the blue bicycle leaning against the front step. "I fixed Josh's tires so he can ride to work today."

"Thanks." Libbie was hopeless when it came to fixing anything.

"Big plans for the Fourth?" He snapped his fingers. "That's right. You've got your sister's party this weekend."

"Technically, it's my parents' party. They just happen to be using Emily's birthday as an excuse." Libbie's younger sister was turning forty-four, and her parents were hosting a party tomorrow evening. Libbie was looking forward to the party the same way she looked forward to her annual pap smear. As much as she adored her sister, she couldn't tolerate her parents for more than a couple hours, and even that was pushing it.

Nick shrugged. "If nothing changes, nothing changes." He knew her family history better than anyone. Better than her own children, really, because she tried to protect them from the complexities of family dynamics. Libbie's relationship with her parents was hers to bear.

"Can you make sure the kids both shower before they show up?" Libbie asked. It was Nick's weekend with the kids and Hercules, but he'd agreed to drop off the kids at her parents' house in time for the party. As far as custody arrangements went, theirs was pretty congenial.

"I'll do my best, but you know they're both stubborn these days."

"Josh will have been out in the sun all day, and Courtney will be covered in sticky ice cream."

Nick grinned. "I'm aware. I stand by my statement."

Libbie couldn't risk the kids showing up a mess. Her mother would have plenty to say about that. "Just drop them off here and I'll take care of it."

Nick ambled along the driveway. "Whatever you want. Make sure they're ready on time today, though. It's going to be busy, and I can't afford to be late opening up."

"I know."

Libbie dashed inside and roused the kids before showering. By the time she rushed out of the house for work, she'd practiced her speech to Joe about twenty times since getting out of bed.

Unfortunately, the drive that normally took half an hour to Basecamp took forty-five minutes, thanks to holiday weekend traffic and an accident that blocked the backroad leading to neighboring Meadowbrook. The stress of the drive was enough to negate the sense of calm that kayaking had provided. Agitated, Libbie hustled into the restaurant. Instead of being early, she was now late.

"You need to plan better," Joe said, as she raced toward the kitchen.

*I can't plan for accidents*, Libbie thought. To her boss she only said, "I know. I'm sorry. There was an accident. Probably someone trying to make a left on Waltham." It had always been a problem spot.

He followed her into the kitchen. "I thought you wanted to talk to me."

Libbie's mind went blank. She was too anxious to think straight. "It's about the menu." That much she could express.

A deep crease formed across his brow. "What about it?" The older man's tone was sharp. Immediately, she was back in sixth grade with Mr. Mason standing over her in gym class, berating her for doing push-ups on her knees.

"I...I thought maybe we could change things up a bit," Libbie stammered as she slipped her white apron over her head. "I have some ideas."

Joe folded his arms. "Ideas? I don't need to change anything. Everything is fine as it is."

"Oh, I wasn't suggesting otherwise." *Only the customers were doing that.* "I just thought we could try something new, as an experiment. See how customers respond."

What had happened to her carefully rehearsed speech? This sounded nothing like it.

"If you want to experiment, do it in your own kitchen on your own time. Now get moving. You know I don't tolerate lateness." Joe turned on his heel and marched out of the kitchen.

Libbie felt as though all the air had been sucked from her lungs.

"I don't know why you bother," Luis said. The porter returned his attention to peeling potatoes. "Joe's an ass. He'll never change and that includes his lame menu."

Libbie stared at the counter, the words she'd painstakingly planned flooding back to her. There was no point in remembering now. She'd blown her chance.

"The ground beef's ready," Luis said.

Of course it was. Another day, another meatloaf.

Libbie pressed her fingers to her temples. It was going to be a long day.

Friday night cocktail club couldn't come soon enough.

# TWO

Libbie parked on the street near her friend Inga's house and rushed to the front door. Thanks to her difficult boss, she was half an hour late for cocktail club and hadn't had time to go home and shower. She knew she smelled like beef and onion. She also knew her friends would understand. If there was one thing this group could do, it was make Libbie feel better about what bothered her. She was safe with these women and she knew it.

Inga Paulsen was an eighty-five-year-old firecracker of a woman who'd moved to Lake Cloverleaf ten years ago from California. She'd lived all over the world, had buried three husbands, and drank and swore like the proverbial sailor. While the other women in the club were in various stages of midlife, Inga had been there, done that, and grew no f*cks in her field. Libbie and her friends had often commented that they wanted to be Inga when they grew up, especially Libbie who envied the older woman's sharp tongue and quick wit. She'd once seen Inga berate a mechanic who'd tried to overcharge her. Libbie had watched, dumbstruck, as Inga walked away with a lower bill and her dignity intact. Six months later, Libbie had remembered that moment when she was overcharged for a tire rotation, but she'd found herself slinking away in silent humiliation, instead of standing her ground the way Inga had.

"Sorry I'm late," Libbie called. She hurried through the foyer with its mismatched antique furniture and back to the kitchen where she assumed the others had congregated. She found them gathered outside on the deck where Inga had installed a bar. By herself, of course, using slabs of reclaimed wood she'd acquired from a local lumberyard and a toolbox that looked older than she did. Inga didn't need an ex-husband to fix bicycles. She was handy enough to do it herself.

"You're here." Kate Golden crossed the deck and greeted Libbie with a half hug. Kate and Libbie had been best friends since seventh grade, when they'd bonded over their shared love of the band Duran Duran. Libbie had always admired her friend's confidence and poise and wasn't at all surprised when Kate started her own business as a life coach. She even had her own YouTube channel and a list of clients from around the world. It helped that Kate had the poise and beauty of a movie star. Throughout their lives, Kate had longed for an interesting life, one filled with different experiences. She'd found a way to make it happen without leaving Lake Cloverleaf, minus the four years she'd spent at the University of Pennsylvania in Philadelphia.

"Traffic is a bitch today," Inga said from behind the bar, pouring Libbie a drink. "Took me half an hour to find parking."

"No bartender tonight?" Libbie asked.

"It's the holiday weekend," Inga said. "I had to elbow my way through the liquor store for supplies. A bartender was out of the question."

"I prefer when it's just us anyway," Libbie said. She felt more comfortable when no one was eavesdropping on their private conversations. Sometimes they shared details of their personal lives that Libbie would hate for others to overhear. She was circumspect about what she shared, of course. She didn't want anyone to think that she was unhappy, and she knew that was how she sounded when she had a few too many cocktails and started talking more openly about her personal life.

"I told Inga it must be a special occasion," Kate said. "She's wearing her necklace."

Libbie turned to admire the pale blue stone with its four holes. She remembered that Inga had worn it the first time they'd met. She'd found the stone along the lakeshore not long after moving to Lake Cloverleaf and decided it was a good omen. A hag stone she'd called it, though Libbie disliked the word 'hag.'

"I consider every Friday night a special occasion." Inga handed Libbie a flute of Prosecco. They always started the evening with a single glass of the bubbly drink before moving on to other concoctions. Libbie couldn't remember when the tradition started, but she enjoyed it immensely.

"Then why don't you wear it every Friday night?" Libbie brought the flute to her lips. She loved the sensation of the bubbles against her skin as she took her first sip.

"Because sometimes it clashes with my outfit," Inga said with a wink.

"How did your talk go with Joe?" Rebecca asked. Rebecca Angelos had been the last one to join their club, after the departure of another woman called Jodie. When Libbie had asked what happened to Jodie, Inga had simply said, "She isn't one of us."

Although Libbie sometimes wondered what she'd meant, she didn't ask.

Libbie had told them last Friday about her plans to speak to her boss. Her cheeks grew warm and she took another sip of liquid courage. She could've used a bottle of Prosecco at work earlier, although the customers might have gotten more interesting dishes than they'd bargained for.

"It didn't," Libbie said. "I was late and then...You know how Joe is."

"He's an ass," Inga said. "That's how he is. All ass, all the time. When he goes to the proctologist, the doctor has to clarify which end is up."

The other women snickered. They were accustomed to Inga's colorful assessments.

"I'll try again next week," Libbie said, knowing that she wouldn't.

Inga thrust a plate of cheese and crackers in front of Libbie. "Why don't you look for another job? You hate it there."

Libbie selected a thick square of cheddar. "I don't hate it there. Basecamp is fine."

"Basecamp is an exercise in abject misery," Inga shot back. "Don't waste your life, Libbie. You're too good for that place."

"She's too good for a lot of things she tolerates," Kate mumbled.

Libbie's stomach knotted. She knew the women weren't fond of Chris. They'd told her more than once she could do better. It was the consensus of her friends that, after three years together, she and Chris should be married or split up. These were the kinds of thoughts the women shared on Friday nights after a few cocktails. It was never mean-spirited, and Libbie knew they had her best interests at heart.

"What are we drinking?" Libbie asked, in an effort to redirect the conversation. She felt too fragile to have her life under a microscope tonight.

"I picked up a new brand of tequila," Inga said. Her blue eyes sparkled behind her thick glasses.

"Tequila and what?" Libbie prompted. She wasn't a huge fan of tequila thanks to a college experience gone awry.

"Mojitaritas, baby," Julie said and clapped her hands for good measure. If anyone needed a mojitarita, Libbie knew it was Julie Duncan. The fifty-year-old lived in a sprawling house on the lake with her bedridden mother, a domineering woman who controlled her daughter's life. Julie had also lost her husband Greg to cancer two years ago. Libbie wished she knew the right way to comfort her friend. She'd read articles until her eyes glazed over, but still nothing seemed appropriate. She didn't want to say the wrong thing and upset her friend further, so she said nothing.

Libbie's mother had attended Greg's funeral and remarked,

rather loudly, how strange it was that Julie didn't cry. As though tears at a funeral were the only acceptable way to express love and sorrow. Libbie had been horrified by her mother's comment. She was often horrified by her mother's opinions and assumptions about people. Delia Stark was the type of woman who seemed to be acutely aware of everyone's flaws, except her own. For someone who never passed a mirror without stopping to admire herself, Libbie found it ironic that her mother was incapable of self-reflection.

"What have I missed so far?" Libbie asked.

Kate smirked. "Rebecca was giving us an update."

The petite brunette groaned. "Day eleventy-thousand and five of my period. The streak continues, literally."

Libbie made a sympathetic noise. Over the past year, forty-six-year-old Rebecca had discovered what the other women already knew—the joys of perimenopause. She'd go months without a period, and then boom! Thirty days straight of spotting. It wasn't a full-on cycle, but it was enough to require a pantyliner and make Rebecca crabby.

"It's not enough for a tampon, which makes the whole swimming thing difficult. Hooray for summer." Rebecca gave her finger a mock twirl in the air. "I feel like all the animals in the shelter know. They stare at me with their big eyes and I can see their pity."

"They're called puppy dog eyes for a reason," Kate said.

Inga gulped down half her mojitarita. "I wish I could tell you it gets better."

Rebecca laughed. "Thanks for the encouraging words."

"No, I mean I don't remember it. It seems like another lifetime ago, as though it happened to someone else."

"There's a silver lining," Kate said. "One day your pantyliners will be a distant memory."

Libbie cringed. "Have we not come up with a new word yet?"

Kate smiled as she took another sip of her drink. "Not everyone has an aversion to the word 'panties' the way you do."

Libbie closed her eyes as she drained her flute. She didn't know why she hated the word so much, only that she did. It was right up there with 'moist' and 'crevice.'

"What about crotch barrier?" Inga suggested. "Is that better?"

"She doesn't like the word 'crotch' either," Kate said.

Julie's nails clicked on the outside of her glass. "You could just call it a liner."

"But then you could be talking about your kitchen drawers instead of your actual drawers. Mentioning floral scented won't help, either." Kate handed Libbie a mojitarita. One of the reasons Libbie enjoyed Friday nights so much, other than the good company, was that no one expected her to make the drinks. In fact, Libbie rarely stepped behind the bar. Someone else was always willing to mix the cocktails. If not Inga, then a hunky bartender that Inga had hired for the evening. Libbie recognized most of the young men from the local bars and restaurants. She suspected that Inga paid well. Besides, Libbie imagined that serving cocktails to five adult women had to be preferable to the boisterous holiday crowd at the lakefront bars.

Libbie inspected the cocktail. "I like the color."

"Go easy," Kate said. "We don't need a repeat of your twenty-first birthday."

Kate had been present for the infamous tequila incident. Her best friend had driven all the way from Philadelphia to Penn State to celebrate with Libbie. It was a good thing, too, because Libbie had to be carried out of the bar that night by two male friends, after vomiting all over the dance floor. Not Libbie's proudest moment.

Libbie took a hesitant sip of the cocktail. "Lime and mint."

Inga winked. "Can't get anything past you."

A cat threaded her way between Libbie's legs. "There you are, Eliza," Libbie said. "I was wondering if I'd see any of you tonight."

Inga had four cats named after the Schuyler sisters—Catherine, affectionately known as "Cat-Cat," Eliza, Angelica, and Peggy. Inga had once spent an entire cocktail club sharing fascinating stories about the Schuyler sisters. Until then, Libbie had only been familiar with Founding Father Alexander Hamilton, not his wife and her sisters.

"The other three were out here earlier," Kate said with a visible shudder. She wasn't exactly an animal person. She didn't like anything that involved extra mess. Libbie had been surprised when Kate ended up giving birth, not just once but three times. In typical Kate fashion, she'd made it look easy and had even bypassed the epidural for the third one.

"They've been climbing all over the fallen tree in the backyard," Rebecca said. "It's too dark to see now, but one of the trees got split in half by lightning the other night."

"It fell clear of the house, thank goodness," Julie added.

Libbie regarded Inga. "I'm glad you weren't hurt, but it's a shame about the tree."

The older woman appeared pained. "The circle of life, my dear. Trees are as vulnerable as we are."

"That tree did better than most," Rebecca said. "It was huge. I bet it was close to a hundred years old."

Libbie knew the exact tree she meant, a majestic oak tree with a thick base and a dozen twisted branches that seemed to reach for the other trees around it.

"Oh, and Kate also shared some exciting news," Julie said.

Kate practically blinded her with a smile. "I hit a million subscribers on my YouTube channel."

Libbie inhaled sharply. "That's incredible. Go you!"

"The secret's out," Julie said. "Now everyone knows what we already knew, that you're an inspiration."

"Not everyone," Kate pointed out, completely serious. "A million other people. That's only a fraction of the number needed for world domination."

"I don't know how you do it," Rebecca said. "Three kids, a husband, your own successful business, and you still manage to have a killer body."

Kate brought her glass to her pale pink lips. "When you love something, it never feels like work."

Inga snorted. "I've been married three times. Trust me, at some point, it always felt like work."

Julie seemed to tower over the older woman as she touched Inga's shoulder. "You've somehow squeezed twenty lives into one. I hope I manage to live even half as much as you have."

Inga's wrinkled lips curled into a smile. "Don't worry, my dear. You will."

A second cat ran up the steps to the deck, its dark coat nearly invisible against the backdrop of the night. Libbie could see the cat had something in her mouth, but only recognized it as a rotten apple when she dropped it at Inga's feet.

"Lucky you, a present," Rebecca said, wrinkling her nose.

"Be grateful it's not a mouse or the head of a bird," Julie said.

Inga took a step back from the apple. "I'd rather it was one of those."

Libbie took a napkin and scooped up the offending item, tossing it into the wastebasket. "Gone now."

Inga continued to stare at the spot on the deck where the apple had been. "But not forgotten," she said quietly.

Julie raised her glass. "This cocktail is pure inspiration. I'm glad you didn't make us one of those special drinks tonight. As much as I love random plants in my cocktail," she said with a roll of her eyes, "this one hit the spot."

"I thought as much." Inga set her empty glass on the bar and waved them closer. "Circle time. Gather around, friends."

Inwardly Libbie groaned. She hated the compliment circle. She was uncomfortable with any form of attention, good or bad.

"I see that face, Elizabeth Stark." Inga wagged a finger at her. "It's important for women to lift each other up."

"I know, I know. It's not that I'm against complimenting everyone else." Libbie dragged herself over to the other women.

"I don't love it, either," Rebecca said.

"It's Kate's favorite time of the evening," Julie said, smiling.

"No, the cocktails are my favorite time of the evening." Kate paused. "But compliments are a close second."

"I feel like I'm back in preschool whenever we do this," Rebecca grumbled.

"That's a good thing," Inga said. "I highly recommend getting in touch with your younger self if you aren't already. Children have much to teach us, especially our own inner child."

Rebecca snorted. "Don't go Mr. Miyagi on us."

"That's not Miyagi, that's Yoda," Julie countered.

"No, the speech pattern is all wrong for Yoda," Kate said.

Inga flashed a look of impatience. "Can we get started before you've named every film from popular culture?"

Kate flipped her blond hair over her shoulder. "By all means. We'll start with Libbie."

Libbie's hands flew to cover her face. "Do we have to?"

"Yes, because you hate it, which means you need more compliments." Kate took a sip of her cocktail and assessed Libbie. "You are the best friend a woman could ask for."

"You are a fantastic chef, and I would eat anything you make," Julie said.

Rebecca smiled at her. "You're trustworthy and responsible."

Inga regarded her with blue eyes. "You're braver than you think and stronger than you know."

"Isn't that a quote from Winnie the Pooh?" Libbie asked. She was sure she recognized it from one of the books she used to read to her kids.

Inga shot her a warning glance. "You know the rules. There's no follow-up to compliments. You can only respond with 'thank you.'"

Kate leaned over and whispered, "It's a variation. Not an exact quote."

Kate would know. With three kids, she'd spent more time with Winnie the Pooh than Libbie had.

They finished going around the circle so that each woman received her share of compliments. Libbie had to admit, as much as she hated the experience when it was happening, she always felt better afterward.

Inga poured another round, and their conversation entered more serious territory, as it often did when the sky was a blanket of stars and a moon as round and bright as a silver coin shimmered overhead. Inga had just finished a story about the death of her second husband, the true love of her life. His death had wrecked her, and she'd been certain she wouldn't last another year without him.

"How did you get through it?" Julie asked, her eyes shining with unshed tears.

"I asked myself one simple question," Inga said.

Libbie watched her closely, trying to anticipate the answer.

"What would Ruth Bader-Ginsburg do?" Kate chimed in.

Inga snorted. "No, but I think that's a reasonable second choice." She sipped her drink. "I forced myself out of bed, finally showered, and then asked myself how could I make that experience the best thing that ever happened to me?"

Libbie winced. How could the death of her true love possibly be the best thing that ever happened to her?

Kate covered Inga's hand with her own. "You make the best of every situation. It's one of the things I love about you."

"Hey, no fair. Compliment time is over," Rebecca said.

Julie downed the drink in her hand. "As much as I hate to break up the party, I need to call an Uber. My mom asked me to be home before ten tonight." She groaned. "I never imagined I'd be fifty years old and still making that statement."

"Why?" Kate asked. "She knows Friday nights are sacred."

Julie met her gaze. "Because she knows Friday nights are sacred."

Libbie sighed into her half-empty glass. It was hard enough that Julie had lost her husband two years ago, but to be caring for an ailing mother too...Libbie knew it wasn't easy. Doris was a challenging woman with unreasonable demands, at least that was Libbie's impression.

"I hope she appreciates what a wonderful daughter you are," Kate said. "When I think of all you've sacrificed to be home and take care of her." She shook her blond head, still perfectly styled and not a hair out of place after a long day.

"She's my mother," Julie said. "It isn't a sacrifice."

"You have a life to live as well," Inga said. "Sitting vigil at your mother's bedside is existing, not living."

Julie shrugged. "Who else will do it? I can't afford a full-time caregiver, not that anyone would want the job. The last part-time person I hired quit after three days."

Libbie knew that story. Doris had cursed and spit and made a general nuisance of herself, until the person quit, and Julie agreed to do the job by herself. It was her mother's way of continuing to control her, even though she was now confined to her bedroom. Greg had been the most understanding husband on the planet. He'd lived in that house with Julie and helped look after her mother until his own illness made that impossible. That was a horrible time for Julie, caring for both of them. Libbie didn't know how Julie had managed to get through those dark days without having a complete breakdown. Libbie had helped out as much as she could with errands, grocery shopping, and, of course, cooking. No matter how much she did, though, it hadn't felt like enough.

"I've offered my help before," Inga said.

Julie smiled. "Thank you, but I don't think a voodoo doll of my mother would solve the problem."

"It might make you feel better though." Inga walked over to the bar and set out five shot glasses. "Before you go, I'd like to make a toast."

Libbie waved a hand in protest. "I don't need a shot. The mojitarita is perfectly fine."

"Nonsense," Inga said. She poured the clear liquid into each glass. "One shot each, and I'll let you off the hook."

Reluctantly, Libbie removed the shot glass from the bar. She'd have to leave her car here tonight, but at least she could stumble home on foot. That was the beauty of a town like Lake Cloverleaf.

Inga raised her glass, and the other women followed suit. "In the immortal words of The Rolling Stones, you can't always get what you want."

"You get what you need," Kate finished.

They tipped back their glasses in unison and drank. Libbie's throat burned as the liquid passed over it. Although it wasn't as smooth as she hoped, it wasn't terrible. She was about to share those very thoughts with her friends when Inga's hand shot out, and she clutched Libbie's shoulder. Her empty glass fell to the deck. The older woman grimaced and doubled over in pain.

"Inga?" Libbie placed a hand on Inga's back. "What's wrong?"

"Is it another spasm?" Kate asked. The older woman sometimes complained of muscle spasms.

Inga slipped to the deck, moaning softly.

It was Kate who had the presence of mind to call an ambulance. In the meantime, Libbie kneeled beside the older woman and checked her breathing. The breaths were weak, but they were there.

"Hang in there, Inga," Libbie said. "An ambulance is on the way."

She hoped that the holiday traffic didn't interfere with its timely arrival. The country mountain roads backed up easily.

Julie dropped down to Inga's other side and held her hand. "Stay with us. We haven't finished emptying your liquor cabinet yet."

Libbie smiled at the comment, although she felt the pressure of tears building behind her eyes. They couldn't lose Inga. Not now. Plenty of women lived to be one hundred these days, and Inga was someone with that kind of stamina. At least that was how she'd always seemed to Libbie. Larger than life, despite her five-foot-four frame.

Kate paced the deck as they awaited the ambulance. She reminded Libbie of a sea captain expecting help from shore for one of her sailors. "You can do this, Inga Paulsen," Kate said. "Stay right here so we can drink together again next week. It's my turn to choose the cocktail. I'll make whatever you like."

Inga's head lolled to the side and she coughed. "Tequila sunrise," she croaked.

Libbie's heart lifted at the sound of the older woman's voice. She leaned over and placed a gentle kiss on Inga's forehead. "I'll have tequila again next week, just for you."

The sound of an ambulance split the quiet night air. "Took them long enough," Kate muttered.

Relief washed over Libbie. Everything would be okay. The paramedics would be here any minute, and they'd save Inga. She smoothed back the older woman's fine white hair. "You're going to be okay."

"And so will you. I promise," Inga said, her voice nearly inaudible.

Libbie assumed her friend was delirious. "Only one of us is flat on the floor, Inga."

Kate's shadow fell over them. "The next time you fall flat on the floor, Inga Paulsen, you'd better have kicked back more than one shot. This is far too lame for a woman of your caliber."

Inga managed a gentle laugh. "I will miss you all." She coughed again. "Remember..."

Libbie frowned. "Remember what, Inga? You're going to be fine. You don't have to miss us because we're right here with you."

"Just as I will always be with you." With great effort, Inga turned to face her. "Breath is the spirit."

With those words, Inga Paulsen smiled and closed her eyes for the last time.

# THREE

Libbie lay in bed with her arms resting at her sides, staring at the whirring blades of the ceiling fan overhead. She'd barely slept a wink, and her eyes burned from alcohol and exhaustion. Chris and Hercules were nowhere to be found, and Libbie welcomed the solitude. Chris had still been awake when she'd arrived home last night, tearful and babbling incoherently about lightning strikes and rotten apples. Eventually she'd calmed down enough to share the news about Inga.

"Mom." Courtney appeared in the doorway, but Libbie's head felt too heavy to turn. "Do you want something to eat? I can make you toast with jam."

"Thanks, honey. I'm not hungry." *Whoosh* went the blades as they sliced through the air above her head. She'd always warned the kids about jumping on her bed. The ceiling was just low enough to create a hazard.

Courtney perched on the edge of the mattress. "I'm sorry about Inga. I know how much you liked her."

Libbie patted her daughter's thigh. "She thought the world of you kids." Inga had said more than once that Josh and Courtney gave her hope for the future.

"Chris says you're still going to work today."

"I have to. It's Fourth of July weekend. Joe won't have anyone else to fill in on such short notice."

"Maybe you should cancel on Grandma."

"I don't think so." Libbie allowed herself a small smile. Even if Libbie had been the one to die, Delia Stark would expect her older daughter to resurrect herself in order to show up on time for the party.

Courtney curled up next to her and tucked her legs closer to her chest. Libbie had spent many nights with Courtney in this very position after the divorce. Her daughter had taken the split harder than Josh. Her son had been as practical and understanding as a child as he was at sixteen. Libbie considered him something of a marvel. Courtney was more like Libbie, with feelings that ran so deep that sometimes it seemed impossible to access them.

"Chris said it was a heart attack," Courtney said.

Libbie nodded. "That's the unofficial word. It happens."

"He said old ladies shouldn't drink. That maybe if she'd started a sewing club instead of a cocktail club, she'd still be alive."

Anger sparked inside Libbie, but she clamped down on it. "Tequila didn't kill Inga, sweetie. She'd crammed a lot of years into those eighty-five. I just think her heart wasn't as strong as her spirit." Libbie frowned. "Hey, you're not even supposed to be here. Does your dad know?"

Courtney nodded and kissed her cheek. "I'm not staying long. I have to write the daily flavors on the board."

Libbie smiled. "Your favorite part, other than taste tests." Her daughter was an artistic child with an eye for detail. Libbie often wondered where her talent had come from since neither Libbie nor Nick was particularly artistic.

"There's coffee downstairs. I told Chris to make extra."

Libbie cupped her daughter's cheek. "Someday, you'll take good care of me in the west wing of your mansion."

It was their little joke that one day Courtney would be wealthy enough to dedicate an entire wing of her home to Libbie's care. She promised herself that she wouldn't be anything like Julie's mother, though. Libbie had no interest in controlling Courtney's life when she could barely keep up with her own.

"Only silver spoons for your tongue, milady," Courtney said.

She rolled to her feet and Libbie realized how grown-up she looked now. Summer at the lake would be different this year for the thirteen-year-old with her adorable figure and engaging smile. Something else for Libbie to worry about.

"Have your dad drop you off here later, and we'll go to the party together," Libbie said. "I need you showered and appropriately dressed."

"He already gave us the schedule." She paused at the sound of thunderous footsteps in the hallway. "Hercules is back."

"You don't say." Before Libbie could shift the covers, the dog leaped onto the bed and dripped saliva on her bare arm. "I guess I'm getting up now."

Courtney blew her a kiss. "I'll see you later. I hope you feel better."

"Thank you." Libbie stroked the dog's fur before padding into the bathroom for a shower. Her head started to throb, and she wished she'd had more water last night. She'd been too distracted. Her late arrival had thrown her off balance and she'd never recovered.

She waited until the warm water splashed her skin, and only then did she give herself permission to cry. Libbie's showers were her safe haven, a place where she could hide from the world and allow herself to feel. It was the place where she'd cried as a young and overwhelmed mother, as a wife in a failing marriage, and finally as a girlfriend in a frustrating relationship. The water washed away her dissatisfaction with her job and family. It was where she'd cried when, in the middle of her divorce, her father had the nerve to call and bemoan the difficulty of her younger sister's life. Emily, who had an intact marriage, a job she loved, healthy children, and four doting grandparents.

Libbie still remembered how she'd felt in that moment. She'd just come from the lawyer's office with both kids in the car because the babysitter had cancelled. The kids had been fighting, and she'd been worried about money and the emotional impact of the divorce on the kids. Her father called and she'd put him on speaker, a move which she later regretted and would never repeat. The upside was that her kids had gone quiet at some point during the call and, when she'd turned around to check on them afterward, she'd seen the look of complete understanding on Josh's young face.

"Why doesn't Pop-Pop ask about us?" Courtney had asked. Her young narcissistic brain had correctly noted Jerry Stark's interest in Emily and her offspring and his lack of concern for Libbie and her kids during such a difficult time.

*Welcome to my world*, she'd thought. To her daughter, she'd said, "I'm sure he does the same to Emily. Calls her and worries about us." Even as she said the words, she knew they were untrue. Her parents had doted on Emily from the moment she was born, relegating Libbie to a footnote in the story of their lives. No matter how well Libbie performed at school or in athletics, it was never enough to hold her parents' attention. Emily simply shone so brightly that Libbie became nothing more than a shadow. A silhouetted branch on the family tree. As aware as she was, it didn't stop her from trying, even now. It had become part of her identity, like her blue eyes and freckles.

As Libbie toweled off and dressed, her thoughts turned to Inga's funeral. The older woman had no family left to speak of, no children or close relatives. Kate was handling the funeral arrangements. Her best friend was invaluable in a crisis, which was ideal for Libbie because her anxiety tended to cause her to freeze up or shut down in difficult situations.

She dressed for work and hurried downstairs for a quick cup of coffee before she braved the Saturday traffic. She looked forward to Tuesday when things would calm slightly, although the summer months always brought more of everything.

More traffic, more people, but also more money.

At Basecamp, the lunch crowd was as busy as she'd anticipated, and Libbie worked herself into a frenzy. Truth be told, she was grateful for the distraction. She only had a single fleeting image of Inga's lifeless face when she was stirring the gravy for the turkey medallions.

By the end of her shift, Libbie's feet and back hurt and she was ready to flop into bed and succumb to emotional exhaustion. The last thing she felt like doing was enduring an evening with her parents, but it was her sister's birthday, and Libbie loved Emily.

Just as she was ready to slip out the back door, Joe intercepted her. "I'm going to need you to cover for Maria on Tuesday."

Libbie faltered. "I'm sorry, Joe. I can't. That's the day of my friend's service."

Joe hesitated, and Libbie thought he was finally going to offer some sort of condolence, which he'd failed to do when she'd first told him the news. Instead he said, "So you were really next to her when she died?"

Libbie's stomach tightened at the memory. "Yes."

"I've never been there when somebody's died."

Libbie stared at him. "I don't recommend it."

Joe dragged a hand through his curly hair. "Well, I don't know what I'm gonna do if you can't sub for Maria."

Libbie's jaw tensed. If he gave her a hard time, she didn't know what she'd do. "What's going on with Maria?"

"She's got an appointment with the plastic surgeon about her new..." He cupped his chest. "It takes months to get an appointment with this guy. That's how good he is."

Libbie cleared her throat, unsure what to say. It wasn't as though Maria was having reconstructive surgery. Apparently, her fiancé had offered to pay for a larger cup size, and Maria decided to take him up on it. "I don't know what to tell you, Joe. It's a funeral service, not a dinner reservation."

His expression registered surprise, and Libbie understood why. Usually she was accommodating, but this was her dear friend Inga's funeral. She couldn't reschedule it, and she had to be there.

"What time's the funeral? How about you come in late or leave early, depending on the timing?"

Libbie's mouth dropped open. Instead of kicking him in the balls the way she wanted to, she heard herself say, "I'll see what I can do."

Her hands shook as she got into her car and drove home.

Libbie's parents lived in a modest lakefront home that they'd purchased after her father's retirement. Libbie exited the car, the familiar tight ball of anxiety forming in the pit of her stomach. It was always this way when she was about to interact with her parents. The air was warm, and the scent of grass permeated the air thanks to an early afternoon rain shower.

"I bet she loves her present," Courtney said. She'd insisted on wrapping the gift in paper that she'd decorated herself with drawings of butterflies. She'd used brightly colored markers laced with glitter so that the images shimmered on the paper.

"I think she'll love the paper more."

Courtney beamed in response, and Libbie was relieved that her daughter didn't downplay her talent. Not today at least.

Delia Stark opened the door with a flourish. She wore a red and white top paired with a blue skirt in honor of the holiday. Libbie noticed that her earrings were little American flags with encrusted diamonds.

"We're here," Libbie said with forced cheer.

Libbie's mother inspected her from head to toe. "You should've gone home to shower after work. We would've waited for you."

"It's fine," Libbie said. Never mind that she had showered and taken great pains with her hair and makeup, knowing she'd have to endure her mother's scrutiny.

"Where's Chris?" she asked, making a show of peering behind Libbie, as though Libbie was actually wide enough to block her mother's view of him.

"He has a friend visiting from out of town for the holiday," Libbie mumbled. She was a terrible liar.

As they stepped inside, Emily rushed forward to embrace her sister. "I am so sorry about Inga. What a terrible loss."

Libbie sank against her sister, grateful to have someone who understood her connection to the older woman. "Thank you."

"Oh, yes," her mother said. "The German woman. I heard the dreadful news."

Libbie bit her tongue. Inga had lived in America since she was a child. She didn't even think of herself as German.

"Why don't you come to the patio?" her mother suggested. "I'm sure these kids are starving. Look at Josh. He's made of skin and bones."

"It's called a growth spurt, Mom," Emily said. "My kids are the same."

Her mother peered at Josh, who was now taller than her. "I don't know. His pallor is a bit green. Has he been for a physical this year?"

"Yes, Mom."

"I'm a lifeguard, Grandma," Josh said. "I had to be cleared."

"Oh, right. You're both working this summer, aren't you?" She turned and walked through the dining room and diagonally through the family room to reach the back door. "Pop-Pop is manning the grill, of course. He'll be happy to relinquish it now that you're here, Elizabeth. You know how he hates the heat."

The last thing Libbie felt like doing after work was standing outside in front of a hot grill, but she smiled and said, "I'll be right there. Let me just say hi to everyone."

'Everyone' consisted of Emily's husband and their two sons, Sam and Ryan. She liked her brother-in-law well enough, but they weren't particularly close.

"Aunt Libbie, did you hear I'm trying out for varsity soccer?" Sam asked. Although he was only fifteen, he'd proven to be as athletic as he was handsome. It hadn't escaped Libbie's notice how much her mother doted on Sam. It was like a repeat of Libbie and

Emily. Josh was her oldest grandson, and Courtney was her only granddaughter, yet she still found reasons to prefer Emily's children to Libbie's own.

"Your mom told me," Libbie said. "That's great."

"I know a couple of guys on the team," Josh said to Sam. "They're really nice."

That was the most interaction Libbie had with anyone at the party. She spent most of it chained to the grill, flipping burgers, and making sure the hot dogs had the black marks the kids liked. It was amazing how many burgers such a small group could inhale. Finally, the orders stopped, and she was able to make up her own plate of food. She sat at the outdoor table to enjoy the meal. Her father sat next to her, talking to Emily's husband across the table about a tennis tournament. The sun had dipped below the horizon, and Libbie watched two fireflies as their lights brightened and faded in sync.

When she'd finished eating, she carried her empty paper plate into the house to dispose of it. She knew how much her mother hated cleaning up at the end of a party, so Libbie made sure to tidy up as much as she could before they left.

As the lid of the trashcan closed, Libbie felt her phone vibrate in her pocket. She expected it to be Chris. To her surprise, it was an unknown number. She let it go to voicemail, and then tapped the screen to listen.

"Hi, my name is Ethan Townsend. I'm an attorney and I'm trying to reach Elizabeth Stark on behalf of the estate of Inga Paulsen. If you could return my call at your earliest convenience, I would appreciate it. Thank you so much."

Libbie studied the number on the screen, debating whether to return the call now. It was Saturday night on a holiday weekend. He probably wouldn't answer. Then again, he'd just called her. What if there was a problem, something connected to Inga or the funeral? She slipped into the bathroom and closed the door before clicking the number on the screen.

"Ethan Townsend."

"Um, hello. This is Elizabeth Stark returning your call."

Someone knocked on the bathroom door. "Libbie, are you in there? We're about to bring out the cake."

She held her hand over the phone. "I'll be right there, Mom."

"I'm sorry to disturb your holiday weekend, Ms. Stark. I just wanted to be sure that I got in touch with you before the funeral. Mrs. Paulsen's instructions were very specific."

"She asked you to call me?"

"I'd like to meet with you before the funeral, if you're available."

The ball in her stomach tightened. "Just me?"

"You and three others."

She relaxed slightly. "Kate, Julie, and Rebecca?"

"That's right. You're all friends, I understand?"

"Yes. Very good friends." Tears gathered in the corners of her eyes. Why couldn't she feel about her own family the way she felt about her friends?

"Would you mind coming by at nine thirty on Tuesday? That should give you enough time to prepare for the service." He gave her the address.

"Yes, of course. I'll be there."

Another knock on the bathroom door. "Libbie, the candles are lit. Let's go. Your poor sister is waiting for everyone to sing."

Libbie tucked her phone in her pocket and left the bathroom. Everyone was gathered around the island in the kitchen, where a vanilla cake was adorned with pastel-colored candles.

"One, two, three," her mother prompted. Her phone was in her hand, capturing the moment. Libbie knew exactly what she'd see later on her mother's Facebook page. *Happy birthday to the best daughter a mother could ask for.* It was the same every year and every year, Libbie felt a pang of hurt. She'd mentioned it to Chris once, who'd told her she was being 'dramatic,' and that all mothers told their kids they were the best. Except Libbie's mother had never written that on Libbie's birthday. Not once.

They sang 'Happy Birthday', and Libbie mouthed the words,

unable to make a sound. The call from the lawyer had rattled her, even though he hadn't said anything bad. She couldn't wait to text the other women and find out what they knew.

Libbie barely touched her cake and hoped no one noticed. It was the type of thing her mother liked to comment on. *I guess it wasn't up to your standards* was a Delia favorite. A far worse crime would be to reject the piece of cake altogether. That led to questions about diets and exercise that Libbie couldn't handle right now.

The moment the clock struck eight, Libbie motioned to her kids that it was time to go. She hugged Emily and wished her a happy birthday one last time before the three of them exited the house.

"Are you dropping us back at Dad's?" Josh asked on the way to the car.

"It's his weekend."

"Harry has been waking up in the night. It's kind of annoying."

Libbie smiled. "At least your time there is limited. Imagine how your dad and stepmom feel."

Courtney fell in step beside her mother. "Are you okay, Mom?"

Libbie cut a glance at her. "I'm fine. Why?"

"Grandma said you seemed even more miserable than usual. I told her it was probably Inga, but she seemed to think it was more than that."

Libbie scoffed. "More than the death of my good friend?" She released a long breath. "If your grandmother was that concerned, she could have asked me herself instead of making the remark to her thirteen-year-old granddaughter."

Libbie immediately regretted saying that to her daughter. She tried her best to shield the kids from her family issues.

Courtney wrapped her arms around her mother's waist. "Emily seemed to like her present."

"Grandma said she saw it on sale in town," Josh added.

Libbie flinched. She had, in fact, bought it on sale, but she wasn't sure why it mattered to her mother what she paid for it. Her sister loved it and that was the important part.

"I guess she thinks true love means paying full price," Courtney said.

Libbie laughed at the absurdity of it, and, yet, there was a ring of truth to her daughter's statement. She opened the driver's side door with a weary hand. "Come on, kids. Let's stick a fork in this day and call it done."

## FOUR

To Libbie's relief, Maria cancelled her appointment with the plastic surgeon after a fight with her boyfriend. That meant Libbie had enough time to shower and dress for the funeral, without being late for the meeting with the lawyer. If there was any kind of work that needed to be done on behalf of Inga's estate, she didn't want the other women to have to handle it alone. She made a mental list of possibilities and felt her stomach clench as she tried to figure out which ones she could tackle. She didn't want to be the weak link in the chain.

Ethan Townsend's office was in a professional complex on Timber Trail. Libbie had been here once before when she'd needed to see a dermatologist about discolored freckles. They were benign, which hadn't surprised Libbie because she was vigilant about sunscreen. When she'd said as much to the dermatologist, Dr. Winston explained that most of Libbie's sun damage had happened in childhood, and there was precious little she could do about it now. The sunscreen would help prevent new damage, of course, but much of the damage happened years ago and might not reveal itself until later in life.

Her friends were already in the waiting area when she arrived. Each woman wore a tasteful black dress but with varying accessories. Libbie had declined to wear jewelry at all, not wanting to look like she'd tried too hard. It was a funeral, not a fashion show.

"I feel like there should be a different dress code for summer funerals," Julie said, plucking the fabric of her dress away from her skin. "Black is the worst."

"You should've worn your pearls," Kate said.

Libbie's fingers drifted to her bare neckline. "I thought about it, but I didn't want to look too fancy."

"It isn't a wedding where you run the risk of outshining a bride," Kate said. "Pretty much everyone outshines a corpse."

"Kate!" Julie's admonishment rang out in the tiny waiting area.

"Oh, please, Inga would've laughed," Kate said.

Their exchange was interrupted by the opening of the office door. A lustrous head of silver hair poked through the doorway. His beard and mustache were neatly trimmed, but his hair was gloriously tousled and fell well past his neck. Libbie hadn't realized she was a fan of his look until this very moment.

"You must be here for Inga Paulsen," he said.

He was what Kate would describe as a silver fox. With his dark blue suit, colorful tie, and healthy glowing skin, he looked like an advertisement for a Successful Adult Man. She immediately conjured an image of Chris in his boxer shorts in the kitchen, standing amidst a mess he'd made but failed to clean up. The Successful Adult Man seemed like the type to wipe down the counters and load the dishwasher after cooking her breakfast. Or maybe that was just Libbie's fantasy of a good partner.

Kate was the first on her feet. She strode forward and shook his hand. "I'm Kate Golden."

"Nice to meet you. I'm Ethan Townsend."

"Julie Duncan."

"Rebecca Angelos."

Libbie was the last one to stand and shake his hand. As his warm hand clasped hers, she suddenly felt inept and couldn't seem to find her voice.

"And you must be Elizabeth," he said, smiling at her.

His eyes crinkled in the corners in a way that was both attractive and infuriating. When Libbie's eyes crinkled in the corners, they were crow's feet, a sign of middle age that she couldn't hide without the help of a plastic surgeon. The Successful Adult Man, however, didn't have to hide. He could flaunt his glossy silver hair and wrinkles with a charming smile, while Libbie's colorist was on her birthday and Christmas card list. Libbie recognized that part of her reaction was due to her internal misogyny. She only knew the term because Kate had brought a book to cocktail club last year that had opened Libbie's eyes to the way women treat each other. She was relieved to learn that she didn't fall into most of the traps, but, as with anyone, there were a few areas ripe for improvement.

"Libbie," she corrected him. "Everyone calls me Libbie."

"Nice to meet you, Libbie." He motioned for them to join him in the office where four chairs were carefully arranged in a semicircle in front of the desk. "I appreciate you coming before the funeral. I know time is of the essence, but Inga was insistent that you receive her assets as soon as possible after her death."

"Why? Did she leave us frozen shrimp or something?" Rebecca slumped against her chair the moment the words left her mouth. "Sorry. I'm terrible in uncomfortable situations."

Libbie patted her thigh. "You are not," she whispered.

Libbie was far worse, except she tended to say nothing at all. She was too afraid of saying the wrong thing, which had the effect of making the other person feel like she didn't care. It wasn't an ideal dynamic.

Ethan opened a file on his desk. "Let's get started so we can get you out of here. I don't want to add to your stress on such an emotional day."

Libbie sighed inwardly. Ethan Townsend seemed more like a compassionate doctor than a lawyer. Weren't they supposed to be stuffy and devoid of personality? That was what she'd gleaned from television, anyway.

He lifted a document from the file. "As I'm sure you know, Inga Paulsen was a witch."

"That's rude," Kate interjected. "She was a lovely woman who lived an incredible life."

The lawyer chuckled. "I'm not casting aspersions, Mrs. Golden. Inga identified as a witch. I thought you knew."

The women exchanged awkward glances.

"Well, we know she was an eccentric woman," Julie said carefully.

Kate leaned forward. "Define witch."

Ethan seemed at a loss for words. "According to Inga, she had certain...abilities." He frowned. "You're sure she never discussed this with you?"

Kate barked a short laugh. "No. I definitely would've remembered a conversation like that, no matter how many cocktails we consumed in a night."

Ethan scratched the back of his head and chuckled awkwardly. "Okay, I guess I'll take things a little more slowly then. Inga Paulsen was a registered witch and, as such, that gave her the right under Article III, Section 2(b) of the Witch's Covenant to distribute her assets as she deemed fit."

Rebecca burst into laughter. "This is a prank, right? Inga paid you to do this after she died." She looked at the other women. "Can't you just see Inga setting this up ahead of time?"

"It's not like she knew she was going to die of a heart attack in the middle of our cocktail club," Kate said.

"She still could've arranged it for an indefinite date." Rebecca turned back to Ethan. "Are you even a real lawyer, or do you rent this place for when you need to perform?" Her eyes widened. "Omigod, are you a stripper?"

Libbie shifted uncomfortably in her chair. That would explain his handsome looks.

Ethan splayed his hands. "Ladies, I assure you this is all very real. If I didn't have a valid law license, I'd have a lot of explaining to do right now, starting with my mother, who's been telling people how proud she is of her son since about 1975."

Libbie suppressed a smile.

"You're in your forties?" Julie asked.

"No, fifties," he said, "but that was around the year my mother was impressed enough to make a fuss. I think it might've been my finger-painting skills."

Kate set her handbag on the floor next to her chair, a move Libbie recognized. Shit was about to get real.

"Mr. Townsend, I consider myself an educated woman," Kate said. "I graduated from an Ivy League institution and have clients all over the world." She offered him an indulgent smile. "Forgive my ignorance, but what is the Witch's Covenant, and why have I never heard of it?"

"No one knows the origin of the covenant, only that it exists, and that women all over the world are both protected by and subject to its provisions." Ethan paused. "As to why you, personally, haven't heard of it, I can only guess that your reading habits don't extend to the paranormal."

Kate straightened her shoulders. "I'll have you know that I read *Twilight*, the same as every other middle-aged woman in America."

"Those were vampires," Julie whispered. "That sparkled."

Ethan smiled. "I'll be honest, this was all news to me when I first learned of it, but the due diligence has been done, and it's all very real."

The women fell silent as they digested the news. Libbie realized she was digging her fingernails into her palm and forced herself to relax.

"What does this mean?" Kate asked. "Inga ran around with sage and performed bonfire rituals in the woods during a blue moon?"

Ethan shook his head. "I can't say with certainty, but I can see Inga doing that and more."

"Probably naked too," Julie added.

"Sounds about right," Rebecca said.

Everyone laughed, which helped ease the tension in the room.

"How is Inga's witch status relevant to us?" Kate asked. "If she wanted us to know, why didn't she tell us?"

"That I can't answer." Ethan threaded his fingers on the desk, and Libbie noticed that he wasn't wearing a ring. She sucked in a breath, horrified that she'd notice such a thing, not only because of Chris but because they were here for such a somber reason.

"Are you okay?" Julie asked.

Libbie nodded. "Sorry, I'm just feeling stressed."

Kate reached over and squeezed her hand. "We all are. It's a tough day."

Libbie knew that Kate was being kind. Her friend never seemed to get anxious or worked up about anything. Even her anger had a precision about it, the way a paring knife deveins a shrimp. Libbie's emotions were more of the tangled-ball-of-yarn variety, complete with frayed edges and loose threads.

"I'll give you the gist of what I know," Ethan began. "Witches aren't born—they're created. There are no familial covens. No genetics involved."

Libbie clasped her hands in her lap, thinking.

"Not born? Is this like a 'which came first, the chicken or egg thing?'" Julie asked.

Ethan continued without answering. "Witches are made from pieces of other witches, their spirits passed from one generation to the next to form a true sisterhood." He grimaced. "I'm so sorry. I haven't had to give this speech before, and I feel like I'm mansplaining sisterhood to four women. I should have practiced out loud to the bathroom mirror."

Libbie bit the inside of her cheek to keep from laughing. She knew that feeling all too well.

"So you're saying Inga wasn't born a witch, but became one later?" Rebecca asked.

"That's my understanding. At some point in Inga's life, she crossed paths with a witch who decided Inga was worthy of receiving her assets someday." He held out his hands. "And, now, Inga is sharing hers with you."

"Is it tax deductible?" Kate asked. "Because we're really close to the next income threshold..."

Ethan chuckled. "It's not that kind of gift, Mrs. Golden. You won't claim it on your tax returns."

"But you said she was dividing her assets among us," Kate said.

Rebecca touched Kate's arm. "Let him finish, Kate. Then we'll ask questions."

"I think you could've had a career as a lawyer," Ethan said, offering Kate an easygoing smile.

"As a matter of fact, I took the LSATs," Kate said. "I decided it wasn't the kind of life I wanted, to be chained to a desk all day." She paused. "No offense."

"None taken. We're a despised group, even without the corporate prisoner references." He referred to the document. "As you know, Inga had four cats. In her will, she's left one to each of you. Eliza to Elizabeth Stark. Cat-Cat to Katherine Golden. Angelica to Rebecca Angelos, and Peggy to Julie Duncan."

Julie dabbed at her eyes with a tissue. "Oh, wow. She left Aunt Peggy to me?"

Libbie looked at her sideways. "You mean Peggy?"

Julie frowned. "I thought she was called Aunt Peggy."

The other women laughed. "That's only because she's always named last in the sentence," Kate said. "*And* Peggy."

"She also left you this." Ethan reached into a desk drawer and produced a glass jar with a fabric-covered lid. It reminded Libbie of jam jars in the country store, except the fabric was dark blue and covered with white stars.

Kate leaned forward and accepted the jar. "An empty jar?"

"She left a note with it." He handed over a sealed envelope, which Kate also accepted on behalf of the group.

"I hope it explains what she wants us to do with it," Kate said.

"Maybe we're supposed to grow a witchy plant in it or something," Libbie suggested. "Then each take turns caring for it."

"That rules me out," Julie said with a laugh. "I'll murder it overnight."

"What if it's for her ashes?" Libbie asked. They knew that Inga wanted to be cremated and her ashes scattered in the forest not far from the lake. It was something she'd mentioned multiple times over the years.

"Why don't we go back to my place and read the letter together before the funeral?" Kate asked.

The lawyer held up a finger. "Actually, she left you the key to her house as well. Bonnie Shellstrop is going to handle the sale, but Inga also wanted you to have the contents of her liquor cabinet before that happens."

Kate laughed. "She knew us well."

"You can leave the key in the drop box after you've finished," he said. "It should already be there."

Rebecca whistled. "Bonnie moves fast."

"No kidding. Have you ever seen her in a bar full of eligible men?" Julie said. "She's like the Road Runner in a tight skirt."

Kate hugged the jar to her chest. "I guess we should head over there now before the funeral starts."

"The cats will need to be fed and the litter box cleaned," Rebecca said.

"I'll be asking for your help later, Rebecca," Kate said. "I don't know the first thing about owning a cat."

Libbie had never owned a cat before, either, only a dog. She felt her anxiety level rising at the thought of Hercules and Eliza living under the same roof. What if he hurt the cat by accident? He was a large, energetic dog. He could injure the cat just trying to play with her.

"So Inga has left us this jar with a note, a cat each, and the contents of her liquor cabinet, and these somehow qualify as a witch's assets," Kate said. "Is there anything else we need to discuss?"

"Oh, I nearly forgot." He reached into another drawer and produced a stack of four books. "There's one for each of you." He dispensed one to each of them.

Julie was the first to flip hers open. "A blank book?" she asked.

"I think it's meant to be a journal," Libbie said. Courtney had an entire collection of half-empty journals with a variety of adorable covers. This journal, however, was exceptionally plain, with a simple black leather cover and no lettering.

"I think so, too," Kate said. "I suggest journals for clients all the time. Helps to focus your thoughts and provides an outlet for feelings."

"So Inga thought we needed this?" Rebecca asked. "How is this one of her assets?"

"I wish I had more answers for you." Ethan passed a document and a pen across the desk. "Now, I'll just need your signatures."

Julie took them and leaned on the end of the desk to sign. "My mother will flip over the cat and not in a good way."

"Who knows? Maybe she'll be good company for your mom when you're not around," Rebecca said.

"Queen Elizabeth herself wouldn't be good enough company for my mother," Julie complained.

Libbie signed next and passed the document to Rebecca.

"If everything you've said is true about witches and sisterhood," Kate began, "then why would Inga choose a man to represent her? It seems to me she would've chosen a female attorney."

Ethan's expression clouded over. "As a matter of fact, she did. Inga had initially hired my sister. Deb and I practiced together."

Libbie remembered that the sign outside had said Townsend & Townsend. She'd assumed it referred to a father and son.

"But not anymore?" Kate prompted.

"Deb died last year," Ethan said, and Libbie noticed that a muscle in his cheek began to pulse. "Inga and I had gotten to know each other, and she asked if I'd continue to represent her. I was honored that she trusted me."

Libbie could see the pain in the man's eyes and wondered if they reflected her own. Loss seemed all around her today, almost suffocating in its relentless presence. A memory flashed in her mind of young Josh in one of those children's pits filled with hard colorful balls. He'd disappeared beneath them, and she'd jumped in to fish him out, petrified that he would be crushed or asphyxiated. That was what today felt like—she was trapped in a pit of soul-crushing balls that could kill her if she didn't find a way out, and she desperately wanted someone to jump in and save her.

"I'm sorry about your sister," Julie said.

Libbie knew she was probably thinking about Greg. It was natural to relate your own sorrow to someone else's.

"Will you be attending the funeral, Mr. Townsend?" Libbie asked.

"Wouldn't miss it," he said. "Inga left quite an impression on me, as I'm sure you can understand. I'd like to pay my respects." He hesitated. "If you think it will help you, I can give you the name of a witch I spoke to after Deb passed. She might be able offer more insight."

Libbie winced when he stumbled over the word 'passed.' He still seemed to be grieving.

"Lorraine was very enlightening," he continued. "She was able to fill in some blanks for me. Maybe she can help you, too. If you're interested, she calls herself the Voice of the Moon Goddess."

"Thank you," Kate said. "We'll keep her in mind." She signed the document and returned it to the lawyer.

Julie glanced at her phone. "I hate to be the spoilsport, but I don't think we have time to stop by the house before the funeral."

"No, you're right," Kate said. "We'll meet at Inga's afterward, okay?" She cut a glance at Rebecca. "The cats will be fine until then. I'm sure Bonnie fed them."

Rebecca took Libbie's hand. Together, they rose to their feet. "My first witch's funeral," Rebecca said. "I'm sure I shouldn't say this, but I'm actually looking forward to it, now that I know."

Kate shot her a quizzical look. "Why? It's not like she's going to jump out of a cauldron and yell surprise."

"No, but maybe something unexpected will happen," Rebecca said.

Libbie wasn't convinced that a funeral was where you wanted something unexpected to happen, but she understood the sentiment of not wanting to sit in public with uncomfortable emotions for any length of time. She'd do it for Inga, though. The older woman had introduced Libbie to worlds she didn't know existed, and it seemed that she was determined to continue educating her from beyond the grave. Her gaze flicked to the sealed letter now stuffed into Kate's handbag. She had a feeling opening that letter was going to be their introduction to yet another of Inga's lives.

# FIVE

The funeral was held at Needham's, a historic Victorian building with gingerbread trim and a striking view of the lake's south leaf. Although it wasn't officially a funeral home, it wasn't unusual for people to host small gatherings there. It seemed strange to Libbie to look out the window and see people enjoying the water as though nothing had happened, as though the town hadn't lost a remarkable member of its community. That was life, though. Tragedies happened, and the world continued to spin on its axis, oblivious to the pain and suffering of its inhabitants.

"Anyone else expecting Inga to rise up out of the casket?" Julie asked in a hushed voice as they viewed Inga's body.

It had taken Libbie a full minute to look directly at her friend's body. Seeing Inga's small frame in its final resting place made the whole thing real, and Libbie wasn't ready for a reality check.

"If she flies away on a broomstick, I'll eat my hat," Rebecca said.

"That one's too nice," Kate said, admiring her black pillbox hat with its truncated lace veil.

Libbie lowered her voice, ready to pose the question she'd been dying to ask since they'd left Ethan Townsend's office. "So are we witches now? Is that what you all took away from the meeting?"

"I don't think so," Rebecca said.

Julie trained a wary eye on the other guests in case they were overheard. "I think we will be, once we've accepted her gifts or assets or fed her cats for ninety days straight until the next lunar event." She exhaled loudly. "I don't know."

"We did accept her assets," Libbie whispered. What they were meant to do with them was anybody's guess until they could open the letter.

"Are you finished yet?" a gravelly voice asked. "Some of us don't have bladders capable of lasting through an entire service."

Libbie turned to look at the old man behind them in line. He wore a faded suit and a tie that was slightly frayed along the edges. She recognized him as one of Inga's neighbors. "I'm sorry, Mr. Francis. We just wanted to say a proper goodbye."

Mr. Francis stared at the casket, his eyes filled with sorrow. "This funeral seems wrong for our Inga."

"Too fancy?" Libbie asked.

"No, too normal," he replied. "The Inga I know would've wanted to be burned on a pyre and sent across the lake in all her fiery glory."

"I think she put in the request, but the town council turned her down," Kate said. "Health and safety hazard."

Mr. Francis chuckled. "You're her cocktail club, right? I've seen you coming and going from the house on Friday nights."

Libbie knew it was because Mr. Francis spent most of his time in a rocking chair on the front porch of his log cabin-style house.

He edged closer. "Is it true she died after too many tequila shots? I'll be honest, that's a pretty tempting way to go."

"She died after *one* tequila shot," Kate said, "but the cause of death was a heart attack, not alcohol poisoning."

"I figured as much," Mr. Francis said. "Her liver was made of titanium. She could drink me under the table any night of the week —and sometimes did."

Libbie stared into the casket, looking for any sign of Inga's witchiness. Was there a tattoo? Any mark that helped one witch recognize another? She reached forward to shift a wayward strand of white hair from Inga's forehead. If nothing else, her friend looked peaceful.

The women said their goodbyes and moved forward to allow other mourners to pay their respects. Libbie noticed Ethan Townsend further back in the line. Their eyes met, and she glanced away quickly, surprised by the butterflies that erupted in her stomach at the sight of him. She was relieved when Kate's husband came over to provide a welcome distraction. Ethan Townsend might be a silver fox, but Lucas Golden was the physical embodiment of the word 'hunk.' Libbie had approved of him from the moment Kate had introduced him as her boyfriend eighteen years ago, and not just because of his good looks. Lucas had a kind heart and a generous nature. He was the ideal companion for Kate.

Lucas kissed his wife's cheek before turning to greet the other women. "No Chris?" he asked, scanning the crowd.

"He couldn't make it," she lied. The truth was, he didn't offer to accompany her. Didn't even inquire after the details. "The kids and I discussed whether they should come, but I decided it would be too much for Courtney. You know how she is. It'd be nightmares for weeks."

"Yeah, same." Lucas raked a hand through his dark blond hair. "Ours would run riot in here and destroy the place anyway."

"Lucas," Kate said in mock outrage. She gave his arm a playful swat. "Our children would never misbehave at a funeral."

"Hey, if there's one funeral where misbehaving would be acceptable, it's this one," Julie said. "Inga would love to know that kids were running amok."

Lucas rubbed his wife's back. "Are you lingering or heading home?"

"We need to stop by Inga's house after this," Kate said. "Which reminds me." Her gaze darted to the other women before returning to her husband. "We now own a cat."

His brow creased. "A cat? How did that happen?" He cocked an eyebrow at Rebecca. "Was this your doing?"

"Not me this time." Rebecca frequently tried to persuade them each to adopt an animal from the shelter, especially when there was one she deemed 'really special,' which was basically all of them.

"Cat-Cat was one of Inga's, and now she's ours." Kate cupped his rugged jaw and drew him in for a kiss. "The kids will be thrilled."

"I'm sure, but I know how you feel about pets," Lucas said.

"We'll talk about it later," Kate said with a tight smile.

Libbie had been on the receiving end of that smile often enough to recognize it as the end of the discussion. "I can drive us all to Inga's if you want to ride over together," she said.

"Sounds good to me," Julie said, and the others agreed.

They left Needham's, and Libbie took a moment to appreciate the sunshine before ducking behind the wheel of her compact SUV.

Julie slid into the seat behind her. "Just so we're clear, I don't want a funeral. I'd prefer a wake."

Kate took her place in the passenger seat beside Libbie. "I'm surprised Inga didn't request a wake. I could see a big party with body shots off the casket."

"That can be yours," Rebecca said from her place beside Julie.

Kate laughed. "Go for it. Be sure to record it for my YouTube channel. My subscribers will go nuts."

Libbie was quiet as she drove along the curved mountain roads that led to Inga's house.

"Are you going to keep Cat-Cat?" Rebecca asked.

Kate turned to look at her. "Why are you only asking me?"

"Because I know how you feel about pets," Rebecca said.

"I can't give up Inga's cat. If she wanted me to have Cat-Cat, then I will." Kate pushed open the door the moment the car came to a stop.

"She's going to need help with that," Julie whispered.

"Who are you kidding?" Rebecca shot back. "She's Kate Golden. She doesn't need help with anything."

By the time they caught up to their friend, she'd already unlocked the front door and was standing in the foyer. Libbie caught her best friend's mournful expression as she surveyed the compact space. Just as quickly, Kate's face returned to its usual state.

"We should've brought boxes," Rebecca said. "We'll have a lot to carry."

"Inga has boxes in the garage," Libbie said. She'd noticed them two Fridays ago when she'd gone to retrieve another case of wine for the bar.

"If there aren't enough, I have plenty I can bring over," Julie said. "I even have a few garment boxes if Bonnie needs them, or whoever's packing up the house. Greg didn't end up having nearly as many clothes as I thought." She laughed. "And I'd always accused him of being a clothes horse. Joke was on me."

One of the cats came tearing down the staircase meowing. "Someone's hungry," Libbie said.

"More like someone's litter box needs to be cleaned," Rebecca said. "I'll go check it out."

"Be quick," Kate urged. "I want to open this letter and see whether we need to have a seance or something."

"That's a psychic," Libbie said.

Kate shrugged. "Can't witches be psychic?" Her face brightened. "Hey, maybe that's one of the assets."

Libbie shuddered. "No thanks. I don't want to be psychic. I have enough issues with my own thoughts without including anyone else's."

They gathered around the coffee table where Kate placed both the jar and the letter.

"Do you think we need the journals?" Libbie asked.

Kate shrugged. "I guess we'll find out in a minute."

Rebecca hurried to join them, trailed by all four cats. Libbie didn't know whether the cats were actually related to each other, but they bore similar markings of brown, black, and white.

Rebecca knelt beside the table. Her knees had barely touched the floor when Kate ripped open the envelope. Libbie leaned forward expectantly.

"Open the jar?" Kate said, frowning.

"That's it?" Rebecca asked. "The letter tells us to open the jar?"

Kate flipped the letter around so the other women could read it. "Open the jar and receive your gifts."

"No explanation? Nothing?" Libbie settled back on her calves, feeling disappointed. She'd hoped for more information from Inga. Then again, the older woman hadn't told them she was a witch when she was alive. Why would she bother now?

Kate blew out a breath. "Here goes nothing. Literally." She twisted the lid off the jar, and a gust of wind rushed through the room, sweeping the letter off the coffee table and onto the floor. A pungent smell filled the air.

Rebecca coughed and waved a hand in front of her face. "Holy smokes. It smells like Inga when she would eat those garlic bagel chips."

"What's the point of bequeathing her bad breath?" Kate asked.

Libbie fell silent, a memory stirring. An uncomfortable memory but one that seemed entirely relevant. "Her last words," she finally said.

"I'll miss you?" Kate asked.

Libbie shook her head. "She said 'breath is the spirit.'"

"So her spirit smells like garlic?" Julie queried. "That's unfortunate."

Kate pinched her nose. "I hope mine smells like roses."

"It depends on who's opening mine," Julie said.

"What's the gift? I'm confused." Rebecca took the jar from Kate's hand and stuck her nose inside.

"I'm starting to think this really was an elaborate prank," Julie said.

Although Libbie didn't think so, she remained quiet because she couldn't offer a better explanation.

As they stared at the seemingly empty jar, Libbie's arms and legs began to tingle. The sensation rippled across her entire body until she shivered from the effect.

"Does anyone else feel that?" Kate asked.

The four women exchanged uneasy glances. "I do," Libbie said.

"Me, too," Rebecca said.

Julie nodded, her eyes rounded. "Does anyone else—?" She halted as the women seemed to realize at the same time that their skin was glowing with a soft white light. Before anyone could comment on it, their skin reverted to normal.

Rebecca stared at her arms, now outstretched. "What just happened? Are we all going to walk around reeking of garlic? Did she hex us?"

"Why would Inga hex us? She loved us," Kate said.

Libbie breathed into her hand and sniffed it. "My breath smells normal."

Kate turned and blew out a breath in her best friend's face. "How about mine?"

"Smells like you gargled with garbage and then rinsed with acid."

The other women laughed.

"Libbie, that sounds more like something Inga would say," Kate told her. "You know that's my normal breath. That's why I brush a few times a day."

Libbie did know. She knew her best friend's brushing habits as well as her own. "It's your one flaw."

"Why isn't there more to the letter?" Julie complained. She held out her hands and examined them. "Is the tingling somehow the gift? A reminder that Inga is always with us?"

"I don't think so," Rebecca said. "The way the lawyer spoke about it...I think there's more to it than that."

"According to him, we're the Dread Pirate Witches," Libbie said.

Rebecca scrunched her nose. "Like the Dread Pirate Roberts in *The Princess Bride?*"

Julie wore a blank expression. "I don't get it."

Libbie felt a rise of excitement. "Remember in the movie, the Dread Pirate Roberts isn't one person. The name gets passed on to someone else when the current pirate is ready to retire." She'd watched the movie countless times with her kids and knew it by heart.

"And, in this case, retiring is...death?" Julie appeared uncertain.

"Yes. Inga died and passed her witch-related assets on to us," Libbie said. "And someday we'll pass our assets on to others."

Kate tapped the letter on the coffee table. "Except we don't know what those assets are, and she didn't seem inclined to tell us."

"I hope I can turn people into toads," Julie said.

"Would you really do that?" Libbie asked. "They might get run over or drown in the lake before you can change them back."

Julie pursed her lips thoughtfully. "Okay, maybe only a few select people."

"I'm not sure about Dread Pirate Witches," Rebecca said. "If we're sharing her spirit, I think it makes us more like soul sisters."

Libbie liked that idea, too. "I don't care what label we use. I just can't sit in this position anymore." Her knees cracked loudly as she rose to her feet.

Rebecca laughed. "I was waiting for someone else to say it first." She used the table to pull herself upright.

"Cramp," Julie moaned and limped to the wall to try to stretch her calf and foot.

"You need more potassium," Kate said. She was the only one able to rise gracefully without a crack or cramp.

Julie craned her neck to look at them, still stretching. "You saying it fifty times doesn't make it true. There's nothing wrong with my diet. It's my knotty muscles."

"Then try yoga," Kate said.

Julie hobbled back to the coffee table. "I'd rather eat a pretzel than be one."

Rebecca smiled. "You crack like a glow stick. Might as well glow like one."

"This is crazy," Julie said. "And we're crazy for going along with it."

"Either way, Inga wanted this. As her friends, I say we roll with it," Kate said.

"Okay, so what now?" Rebecca prompted.

Kate glanced to the doorway. "I guess we should divide the contents of the liquor cabinet. Those are the real assets."

"And the cats," Rebecca said, inclining her head toward the couch where all four cats were now asleep.

"I have a question," Libbie said. "How did she get her spirit, or whatever it is, into the jar before she died? Does that mean she gave it up early?"

"You're thinking too hard about this," Kate said. "The more I think about it, the more I think the jar was meant to be symbolic."

"Then how do you explain the tingling and the smell?" Libbie countered.

"It's like that psychology experiment when a group of people think they've experienced the same event, but they all imagined it." Kate snapped her fingers.

"No, I definitely felt something," Libbie said. There was no way she'd imagined it.

"I'm not sure," Rebecca said. "Maybe it was something like mass hysteria."

"We *glowed*," Libbie insisted. "We all saw it. There's no point in denying it now."

"If anyone manages to turn someone into a toad, let me know." Kate swept her handbag off the floor and slung it over her shoulder. "In the meantime, I call dibs on the tequila."

## SIX

Libbie was glad she'd thought to ask Rebecca for advice on the best way to introduce Eliza to Hercules. It was handy having an expert on speed dial. Courtney was thrilled to meet the new member of the household and seemed to claim her as her own from the moment Libbie walked through the door, which worked out because Eliza's introduction to the household involved confinement to Courtney's room. Rebecca had instructed them to feed Eliza on one side of the bedroom door and Hercules in the hallway on the other side of the door so each had a chance to get used to the other's smell.

"You're not actually going to keep it, are you?" Chris looked at her askance from the kitchen table.

"Keep *her* and, yes, that's the plan." Libbie opened the cabinet for a glass and filled it with water. She felt thirsty, as though she'd been outside inhaling dusty air all day.

"We didn't agree to a cat. You should've asked me first."

Libbie swallowed a mouthful of water. "I didn't exactly plan for my friend to die and leave me a cat in her will." She noticed a dirty pan on the stove and realized that he'd eaten dinner without her. "Would it have killed you to cook enough for me so that I don't have to make something?"

Chris looked startled by the question. "I guess I didn't think about it."

"I always cook enough for you. Why wouldn't it occur to you to do the same for me?"

His mouth opened and closed, like a fish on a hook. "What's gotten into you? Are you upset about your friend? I know it's not your period."

Libbie glared at him. "Of course, I'm upset about my friend, but that's not what this is about." Libbie listened for a moment to make sure her daughter wasn't within earshot. "I think you take me for granted. I think it would be nice if you made me breakfast on occasion, or any meal for that matter. I think it would've made sense for you to get a job this summer, even if it was part-time. We're not destitute, but we're not exactly growing money on trees, either."

Chris narrowed his eyes. "Are you drunk?"

Libbie resisted the urge to grab the dirty pan from the stovetop and hit him over the head with it. "No, Chris. I'm not drunk. I'm communicating my feelings, something I should've been doing long before now."

Chris pushed back his chair and stood. "I'm not in the mood for this."

"You've had a three-year grace period, and that's on me, but I'd like to discuss it now." She leaned her back against the counter, the sound of her heartbeat thundering in her ears. "This doesn't have to be one-sided. If there's any issue you'd like to raise, I'll listen."

He swaggered toward her. "The only issue I'd like to raise is when did you become such a nagging bitch?" He didn't await a reply. He simply turned and stomped out of the house.

"That's it?" she called after him. "I voice my opinion once in three years and you're opting out of the conversation?"

Was their relationship really that fragile that the second she asserted herself, he was gone? She continued to stand there, rooted to the floor, until she felt a tickling sensation on her ankle. She glanced down to see Eliza weaving between her feet.

The cat looked up at her. "Meow."

"Meow, indeed."

Eliza jumped onto the counter and knocked into the blank book Libbie had received from Inga.

"That's a good idea, Eliza. If I can't communicate my feelings, I can write about them." Libbie opened the journal, intending to write her first entry. To her surprise, the first page was no longer blank. She blinked rapidly, wondering if she'd somehow skipped over this page when she'd first received the book.

Eliza dipped her head to examine the page, and Libbie gently shifted her aside for a better view. "A cocktail recipe?" It seemed appropriate, although there was no title, and she didn't recognize what the result would be from the ingredients.

She checked the cabinets to see if she had all the necessary items. Then she remembered the box with her share of Inga's liquor cabinet and went in the garage to investigate. She was pleased to find a bottle of light rum as well as dark rum. Another ingredient she recognized—only because it grew in her garden—was *Osmunda regalis*, the Latin name for Royal Fern or Flowering Fern. Libbie wouldn't have thought to add a plant like that to a cocktail, but, she knew that if Inga had anything to do with the recipe, then it would be a masterpiece. She snipped off a frond from the fern flowering in the garden, added it to the simple syrup recipe, and let it steep for twenty minutes after boiling. Two teaspoons of lime juice would round off the recipe.

"What are you making for dinner?" Courtney asked. She sniffed the air as she drew closer to the stove. "It smells sweet."

"This isn't dinner, honey. It's a recipe that Inga left for me. I thought I would honor her by making it now."

Courtney smiled. "I think she'd like that."

"I'm sorry it's so late. Let me see what I can whip up."

"What about Chris?"

Libbie realized that she'd been so intent on the recipe that she'd forgotten all about her uncomfortable confrontation with Chris. "He already ate."

"Should we wait for Josh?"

"He won't be home until late. He was going over to Hugo's after work."

Courtney gripped her mother's arm. "Can we have breakfast dinner? Please?"

Libbie glanced at the pan of simple syrup that was now cooling. "Sure, why not?" She made a cheese omelet (that seemed more cheese than omelet) and sausages, Courtney's favorite. She watched as Courtney heaped ketchup all over the food. She'd never seen anyone as enamored of ketchup as her daughter. She pictured her as a grown woman, squeezing two teaspoons of ketchup into her cocktails. She'd probably love a Bloody Mary, although Libbie wasn't a fan.

After dinner, Libbie removed the fern leaves from the syrup, combined the ingredients in a shaker, and strained them into a small rocks glass over ice. She settled on the patio and took her first sip as a setting sun filtered ribbons of brilliant pink and orange through the trees. She sat there until she was bathed in darkness and marveled at the diamonds fixed in the sky. Hercules sprawled at her feet and, at some point, Eliza appeared and curled up in her lap. Josh poked his head outside to say he was home and going to bed. Libbie said good night, her empty glass still clutched in her hand. Her mind was elsewhere, a place she didn't recognize but was content to dwell there for the evening. By the time she re-entered the house, it was clear that Chris wasn't coming home tonight. It occurred to Libbie as she changed into her pajamas and brushed her teeth that she didn't really care.

Libbie woke up the next morning feeling more energized than she had in years. She felt *good*. There was, of course, the empty space in the bed beside her. She didn't think to check her phone until she was downstairs eating breakfast. There was one text from Chris.

Is this a mood swing?

Libbie deleted the message without responding. She'd deal with him later. She stuck to her routine, taking the kayak around one leaf of the lake, and returned to shower and dress for work.

"You're in a good mood," Josh said. He'd caught her whistling as she enjoyed a second cup of coffee.

"I had a good night's sleep," she said. In fact, she had. No insomnia. No bad dreams. Just blissful slumber.

"I didn't," Courtney said. "I could hear all the crickets."

"Then sleep with your window closed," Josh chided her.

"I like the breeze when it's not humid."

"Then don't complain about the crickets."

Libbie was barely conscious of their bickering. She felt alive and very much in her own skin. She didn't know how to explain it any better than that.

On the drive to work, she even rolled down her window and sang along to the music without worrying whether any passing drivers would laugh at her. The traffic gods had smiled upon her today. There were no accidents or traffic jams and she hit every green light between home and Basecamp.

She strode through the restaurant with an air of confidence she didn't realize she possessed. She was going to try again to speak to Joe. She'd even come up with an idea on how to improve the meatloaf recipe without ditching it completely if he was too afraid to make a drastic change, although she truly felt that a drastic change was what Basecamp needed to survive. She'd heard enough customer feedback and listened to Joe's complaints about profit and losses to know that much.

"Hey, Libbie," Luis greeted her.

"How are you today, Luis? Is Joe around?" she asked.

"Not yet."

Libbie set aside her disappointment and got to work. She decided to make one of her own recipes before the kitchen got too busy, so that Joe could sample it for himself and decide. She figured he'd be more receptive to actions than words.

By the time business picked up, Libbie had managed to finish her spin on meatloaf and kept it warm for whenever Joe decided to grace them with his presence. She brightened when he finally entered the kitchen on the way to his office.

"Joe, do you have a minute?"

He halted to look at her. "What's up? You're not going to ask for another day off, are you? Because I don't have time to fiddle with the schedule."

"No, I'd like you to try something." She grabbed a pot holder and removed the dish from the warming drawer. "I've been working on some new recipes that I think would be great additions to the menu."

His gaze darted to the dish in her hand. "What is that?"

"It's a new take on classic meatloaf. I thought it might be nice to shake things up a little. Excite the customers' palates." She set the plate on the counter between them. "Try it and let me know what you think."

Joe didn't move for a fork. In fact, he didn't move at all. "What's wrong with classic meatloaf?"

At this point, Luis and the dishwasher took the opportunity to slide out of Joe's view.

Libbie stood her ground, determined to get through her pitch this time. "Nothing's wrong with it. It's just that I have a lot of exciting ideas for the menu, and I think it would be a nice change to stretch our limits a little. See what the customers think, but first I'd like to know what *you* think." She nodded to the meatloaf, which looked pretty damn good from where she stood.

Joe folded his arms and pinned her with a menacing look. "Listen up, buttercup. I'm the king of this castle, you get me? If I tell the serving wenches to deliver ale, they deliver ale. If I tell the kitchen wench to make my meatloaf my way, she makes a goddamn meatloaf my way, and she doesn't say boo about it." He shook a chubby finger at her. "Seen not heard, remember that."

Libbie didn't hesitate. Maybe Joe was afraid to make a drastic change, but she wasn't. Not anymore. "I'm nobody's wench." She removed her apron and tossed it at her boss. "I'm done."

"You're not done," Joe said. "I own this place, and I say when you can leave."

"You own this place, but you don't own me. I quit."

Joe gaped at her. "You can't quit."

"Of course I can. I just did."

He glowered at her from beneath his prominent brow. "When you finish your shift, then I'll fire you. In the meantime, put your apron back on. There are customers out there waiting for their food."

"Then I guess you'd better figure out how to make it because I'm no longer employed here." Libbie walked straight out the kitchen door that emptied into the parking lot and up to her car, her legs moving with long, confident strides. When she opened the door and slid behind the wheel, she expected her hands to be shaking, but they weren't. They were perfectly still. Libbie was in control of her body. Of her life.

She sat in the car and replied to Chris's earlier text.

> Not a mood swing. A mood makeover. Btw, quit my job. See you at home.

Smiling, she started the car and drove away, leaving Basecamp behind.

# SEVEN

Libbie stopped by Kate's on the way home, desperate to share the news with her best friend. She barely made it through the door before the words came tumbling out. By the time they reached the kitchen, Libbie had finished. It was only then that Libbie noticed Kate's perfectly styled hair and makeup.

"I didn't interrupt a recording, did I?" she asked, not that there was anything she could do about it now.

"No, it's fine. I'd just finished."

Libbie stood on Kate's brick patio with a glass of unsweetened iced tea and admired the view of the lake. It didn't matter how many times she'd been here over the years, she always stopped to appreciate the unique vantage point. Kate's house was nestled on an inlet between two of the lake's 'clover leaf' formations, so she had a more expansive view than most.

Libbie drew a long breath to make up for the breaths she'd failed to take while speed-talking her way through the story. "Sorry, I know I should've texted first. I was just so amped up."

"That's understandable. I mean, it's a big deal. You've worked there for years."

"I know, right? How many years have I wasted on Joe? On

Chris?" Libbie had spent years trying to make herself count. To be seen and heard. No more.

Kate leaned her elbows on the island. "I don't mean to burst your bubble, but I'll ask you what I ask all my clients when they want to make a life change—how are you going to pay bills? Insurance?"

"The kids and I are still covered by Nick's insurance," she said. That was one good thing her lawyer had insisted on during the divorce proceedings. "I've been making regular deposits into savings. It's not a lot, but it should be enough to get me through the summer while I get set up."

"Set up? You sound like you already have something in mind."

Libbie squared her shoulders. "I do. I thought of it on the drive home. I've been wanting to create my own dishes for ages, right?"

Kate nodded. "You must have an infinite number of menus by now."

"Right, so I'll start my own catering business. You know how busy summers are at the lake. Families don't want to cook. They're here to relax and enjoy their time together. I can help them with that."

Kate studied her. "Is this because of Inga's death? Are you having some kind of midlife crisis?"

"No, why would you even suggest that?"

"I don't know. You're fighting with Chris. You quit your job. What's next—a sports car?"

"I don't know what's next." Libbie flung out her arms. "Isn't that exciting? I don't know what's next, and I'm not panicking! I'll try the catering thing and see what happens. If it fails, I'll figure out something else."

Kate inched closer to place a motherly hand on her friend's forehead. "No fever."

Libbie swatted her hand away. "I thought you'd be happy for me."

"I am, I swear, but I'm also worried about you. This isn't the Libbie I know."

Libbie flicked a dismissive finger. "That Libbie is gone. She's like good girl Sandy in *Grease*."

Kate folded her arms. "If you strut through town in black leather and heels, I'm staging an intervention."

"Why? What's wrong with that?"

"Sandy changed for Danny, remember? We loved the movie, but we hated that part."

Libbie remembered it well. She also remembered thinking that Rizzo was the most authentic character in the movie.

"Well, good news," Libbie said. "I haven't changed for a guy. In fact, thanks to new Sandy, I'm not sure I even have a guy anymore."

"I hope you're right about that last part because he wasn't worth having. The best thing I can say about Chris is that he isn't a serial killer or a rapist, which is about as low as my bar goes."

Libbie let that sink in. Those were hard words to hear from her best friend, but she wasn't surprised by how strongly Kate felt. "He's definitely neither of those things."

Kate's expression softened and she hugged her friend. "You know I'll support you, no matter what, even if you want to work things out with him."

"I know, and that's why I love you."

Kate pulled back. "What do you think your parents will say? They're going to flip out."

"They'd have to care enough to flip out. They'll probably just criticize me and move on to something wonderful about Emily or her kids. Or some woman at the club whose daughter's friend is a hat model for QVC." There was always someone more interesting than Libbie as far as her mother was concerned.

Kate squeezed her arm reassuringly. "I'm happy for you, Libbie. You deserve all the good things. You know that."

Libbie knew that Kate was resisting her guru-speak, as Libbie sometimes called it. Sometimes it was difficult having a best friend whose entire career was built around being a self-help and motivational guru. Libbie wanted to feel like a friend, not a client, and mostly she did.

"I know you've always said that, but I feel like I'm finally starting to believe it." Libbie hesitated. "Have you noticed anything different about yourself?"

Kate cocked her head. "What do you mean?"

"I don't know. You don't feel...like a better version of yourself or anything?"

Kate tipped her head back and laughed. "Hardly."

"I know, I know. Hard to improve on perfection."

Kate's smile faded. "That's not what I meant."

"Hey, that reminds me. Did you notice anything in your journal?"

Kate's face was blank. "Journal?"

"The book Inga left you. I thought mine was blank, but then I found a page with a cocktail recipe."

"Really? No, as a matter of fact, I looked through mine this morning. Ava wanted to see it. I told her she could, but only if she swore not to use it as a drawing pad." Ava liked to draw like Courtney, but as Kate liked to say to Libbie, double the drawings with half the talent. To be fair, Ava was only six.

"I made the drink last night," Libbie said. "It was amazing. I'll have to make one for you next time."

"That's strange. I wonder why yours had a recipe." Kate frowned. "The lawyer distributed them at random, so it isn't like yours was designated for you."

"You're right." Libbie had forgotten that. "Maybe it was a book Inga had started but didn't get to finish."

Her phone buzzed, and Libbie noticed a text from Chris.

Libbie stared at the words on the screen. Her throat suddenly felt dry.

"What's wrong?" Kate asked.

"Chris is at the house," she said. "He says he's getting most of his things, and he'll be back for the rest another time."

He'd also called her stupid for quitting her job in the middle of summer, but she omitted that part, knowing it would send Kate off on a fiery tangent.

Kate shook her head in disgust. "Unbelievable. All because he didn't want to have an authentic conversation."

Libbie drank the rest of her iced tea, letting the text settle. "Maybe he's worried about both of us being home at the same time all summer."

"It's not like you're going to lie around eating bonbons. You're going to start your catering business."

Libbie was still stuck on the text. That he didn't even have the decency to wait and talk to her in person. "I didn't realize there were two cowards in the relationship." She'd thought she was the only one.

"How do you feel? Do you want to head home now and try to stop him from leaving?"

Libbie leaned back in the chair and adjusted her sunglasses. "I think I'll hang out here for a little while longer, if that's okay with you."

Libbie arrived home an hour and a half later. There was no sign of Chris's car in the driveway, but the mail truck was just leaving, so she stopped at the mailbox before she pulled into the driveway. Chris had been the one to bring in the mail and handle the bills. Libbie made a mental note to make a list of the bills and their due dates. There'd only been a short period of time between Nick and Chris where Libbie had handled everything. She didn't look forward to taking over again. Although some bills arrived electronically and were paid automatically, a few of the main ones sent paper copies, and then Chris paid them online directly from the bank account.

"Lucky me. And here's one now," Libbie said, as she glanced at the envelope from her mortgage company. It seemed different from the normal statement and payment coupon, and she assumed it was one of those offers to switch to a new type of loan that she routinely ignored.

She carried the small stack of envelopes into the house and set them on the kitchen counter. Hercules bolted into the room to greet her, his tongue hanging out the side of his mouth. He always seemed so happy. She wondered what he thought about, especially when no one was home. She'd seen videos of pets sitting in the same spot in the evening as when their owners left in the morning, and they tore at her heart. At least Hercules seemed to enjoy himself no matter what.

She opened the back door to let him out and then remembered to call for the cat. Eliza would take some getting used to. The cat appeared as if out of nowhere, twisting around her legs, her soft tail tickling Libbie's exposed skin. She made sure the cat's bowls were full and then went upstairs to see whether Chris had, in fact, moved out. Dresser drawers had been left half open, and a quick peek in the closet revealed that he had. Libbie took a deep breath in and exhaled slowly. He was well and truly gone. Their relationship had been hanging by a thread so fine that she hadn't even registered its existence.

She returned to the kitchen with Eliza beside her. The cat jumped onto the counter and scattered the pieces of mail. Libbie pulled them into a pile and opened the one from the mortgage company first. The sooner she looked at the marketing material, the sooner she could toss it into the recycling bin. As Libbie scanned the contents, her fingers tightened on the edges of the letter.

It wasn't marketing material.

Ice traveled down her spine and shot through her veins as she read the letter a second time. Three months in arrears? How was this possible? As far as she knew, the mortgage was getting paid each month, just like all the other bills. If it wasn't, there'd be a lot more money sitting in the account right now. Unless...

She dug into her bag and pulled out her phone, her hand trembling as she scrolled to his name and tapped the screen. Voicemail. Libbie drew a steadying breath and waited for the beep.

"I'm sorry, but the voicemail box you're trying to reach is full."

Libbie nearly screamed into the phone, not that it would've done any good. Her heart pounded as she shot off a text to Chris and asked him to call her as soon as possible. If he suspected that she knew what he'd done, she had a feeling he'd be in hiding for as long as possible.

Slowly, she lowered herself onto a chair. Now that the idea had taken shape, there was no doubt in her mind about what happened. Chris had been taking the money intended for the mortgage and using it for his own purposes. How could he do such a thing? Didn't he realize it would eventually come to light, and then what?

Libbie knew what. He'd twist the facts and make it seem like Libbie's fault, and she would've acquiesced. Anything to keep the peace. To not push the limits of what their relationship could handle.

Anything to please him so that he'd love her enough to stay.

The irony, of course, was that he was already gone, and Libbie wasn't the least bit sorry. She hadn't even pushed the limits. She'd simply opened the channels of communication, and that had been enough to send him packing.

No, wait. It was only *after* she told him that she'd quit her job that he'd announced he was moving out. Now that she'd no longer be a source of revenue, he was gone.

Libbie checked the savings account and discovered there was barely any money left in there, too. Enough to keep the bank from closing it, which would have alerted her to his misdeeds. She felt like an idiot for trusting him. For falling into the trap of letting a man handle things for her that she could've done for herself. This was her house. It had been her bank account. Why had she let him control things that already belonged to her?

Because she loved him, of course. Or at least she thought she did. She felt very confused right now.

Her gaze drifted to Inga's book still on the counter. She thought of the special cocktail and the jar and the strange tingling sensation. What if this was some kind of test that she had to pass before she could claim her share of Inga's assets? What if she'd been cursed? She'd felt so good this morning, like a whole new Libbie. No, a better version of Libbie.

Now she felt like her world was about to collapse on top of her.

She barely had enough money to make it through the month. How would she explain this to her kids? Her hands shook as she glanced again at her phone. Yesterday, she'd believed Chris's worst vice was his inconsideration. Now she knew he was also a liar and a thief. The knowledge didn't make her feel any better.

Libbie fingers traced the outline of the phone as she tried to remember the name of the witch the lawyer had mentioned during their meeting. Luna? No, that was a Harry Potter character her daughter liked. Loretta? Even her memory was cursed these days, although she blamed perimenopause for that. She texted Kate and asked for the name, knowing her friend would remember. Libbie was convinced that Kate was skipping menopause all together and going straight to goddess. Knowing Kate, she was feigning her ailments to fit in with the other women. The reply was immediate and, naturally, correct.

**Lorraine. Voice of the Moon Goddess.**

Libbie searched online for a phone number and address. Lorraine wasn't far, only twenty minutes by car. The problem was that her friends would likely have questions, too, once they knew what had happened to Libbie. She decided to make it easy for everyone. Her conversation with Lorraine was brief and to the point. She clicked off the phone, satisfied with the arrangement. If her life was falling apart, then maybe a witch was exactly what she needed to put it back together. She wouldn't need to wait long. Friday night was just around the corner. Inga might be gone, but it looked like there would be five women present at cocktail club after all.

. . .

With the help of her daughter's graphic design skills, Libbie wasted no time creating attractive menu options and a logo for her catering business. She was pleased when Nick agreed to help spread the word at Cone Hut. She didn't expect her ex-husband to use his business to help hers.

"The kids told me about Chris," Nick said. He'd stopped by to drop off flea and tick pills for Hercules that he'd picked up from the vet's office. He was as good about shared custody of Hercules as he was about the kids.

"These things happen," Libbie said vaguely. She didn't want him to know the appalling details. She was too embarrassed. She tucked the box of pills in the medicine cabinet in the kitchen.

"It's because you jumped," he said.

She turned to look at him. "What are you talking about?"

"From me to him. You jumped."

Libbie frowned. "I didn't jump. We'd been divorced for a year when I started dating Chris."

"But you didn't even pause to think about whether or not he was good enough for you. You just went along with it."

She put a hand on her hip. "When did you become privy to my deepest thoughts?"

"Don't be mad. It's a compliment, really."

"Telling me how bad I am at relationships is a compliment?"

"I'm not trying to be unkind. I just thought I could say what I think now that he's not in the picture. I never wanted to say it before because you'd think I was only being bitter or spiteful."

"I wouldn't have thought that, Nick." Her ex was a lot of things, but bitter and spiteful weren't among them.

"Just for the record, the kids are glad too. They didn't hate him or anything, but they didn't like him much."

Guilt gnawed at Libbie's insides. She'd tried to create a safe space at home where her kids would feel comfortable telling her whatever was on their minds. "I'm glad they talked to you about it."

"They're good kids, Lib. We're doing well for a couple of clueless people."

She laughed, remembering their early struggles as parents. "I guess not everything is falling apart." Her smile evaporated as a question occurred to her. "Why would you say that I jumped when you're the one who got married and had another baby?"

He gave her a sheepish grin. "Oh, I jumped, too, but I got lucky. My wife isn't an asshole. It could easily have gone the other way."

Libbie laughed softly. "Why didn't we talk like this when we were married?"

"Because we were both too afraid of upsetting the apple cart. It's an accomplishment that we managed to get divorced, to be honest. We could've easily stayed married another fifty years, secretly miserable but telling everyone we were fine."

"Thank you for divorcing me," Libbie said, smiling.

He bowed. "And thank you for divorcing me. One decision that we both got right. Let me know if you need help with anything now that Chris is gone. I'm happy to help however I can. Anything to make it easier on the kids."

For a fleeting moment, Libbie considered asking for a small loan, but she quashed the thought as quickly as it had bubbled to the surface. This was her mistake and she'd figure out the solution on her own. Besides, Nick had a wife and a third child and he already paid for half the expenses related to their two kids. Libbie would manage. She had to. And she knew exactly what she needed to do next.

Libbie entered the sterile office of the mortgage company and the familiar tendrils of anxiety began to uncurl in her stomach. Worries and what-ifs circled inside her head like a whirlpool, and she struggled to remain focused on the meeting ahead.

She checked in with the receptionist and was advised to take a seat. She'd worn a suit for the occasion and silently cursed Chris for making her don long sleeves and layers in the middle of summer. The longer she waited, however, the more she felt her anxiety ebb away. She was surprised by her own reaction. This was the type of situation where she should be close to tears by now. Instead, she was calm, and her head was beginning to clear. By the time the loan officer appeared, Libbie felt completely in control again. Whatever needed to be done, she would do it.

"Elizabeth Stark?" he asked.

She rose to her feet and offered a confident smile. "Yes. That's me."

"Larry Jefferson. Nice to meet you."

They shook hands, and she followed him back to his office. There would be no waterworks. Libbie would simply explain the situation and ask how to proceed. Maybe she wouldn't need Lorraine's magical assistance. Maybe she'd be able to take care of this the old-fashioned way. Still, if there was going to be any further unraveling of the careful threads of her life, Libbie wanted to know so that she could put a stop to it. She wasn't certain how much more she could take.

Once they were ensconced in his office, he tapped the computer mouse. "Three months, Ms. Stark."

"Yes, I know." *Now*. "I'm not here to offer excuses. I just want to know what I can do."

"Aside from pay what you owe right now?" he asked, not unkindly.

"Unfortunately, that's not an option." She gripped the handle of the bag resting on her lap and noticed that her palm wasn't sweaty. Baby steps.

"You've been a customer in good standing for years, until recently, of course. We're willing to work with you to help you get through whatever hardship you're facing."

"Seriously?" Libbie hadn't expected it to be that easy.

"Within reason," he added. "There are a few options. We can set up a repayment plan, or there's forbearance, or we can modify the terms of your existing loan." He went on to explain each option in greater detail.

Libbie digested the information. "And what happens if I don't come up with the money?" She hated to even ask the question.

"I think you probably know, Ms. Stark. We'd have to foreclose on your house."

His answer jarred Libbie. As much as she wanted to blame Chris, she knew she was also to blame for putting her trust in the wrong person.

Never again.

"The thing is, I quit my job. I wouldn't have done that if I'd known what was going on, of course." But she didn't, and she refused to beat herself up over it now. What Chris had done with the money was anybody's guess.

"You didn't know you weren't paying your mortgage?"

She waved a hand. "The details aren't necessary."

"Maybe forbearance is the way to go," Larry said. "We can freeze your payments now, but you'll still need to pay it all back. Given that you've already missed three payments, I don't think it would be wise to offer you more than two more months. You don't want to end up in a hole so deep you can't climb out."

Libbie silently agreed. "At the end of the forbearance period, what happens? I have to pay a lump sum?"

"Or we can set up a repayment plan where we add a certain amount past due to each new payment as it comes due. Or we can modify the terms of the original loan."

Libbie couldn't foresee being able to pay a lump sum, and she didn't want to modify the original loan. She'd thought long and hard before choosing that particular one and didn't want to extend the term.

"I'll go with forbearance and then a repayment plan," she finally said. She only hoped that she was in a sturdy enough financial position by then to make the payments. She was going to have to cater every opportunity that she could find. Children's parties. Retirements. Hell, she'd cater a Boy Scout picnic if it helped her pay the bills.

Larry printed out the paperwork, and she signed, her heart fluttering with each stroke of the pen. She could do this. Whatever happened next was within her control. She thanked him profusely as she left, relieved that she was being given a chance to make things right. They'd get their mortgage money and she'd keep her house. A win-win.

Her next stop was at the bank, where she removed Chris's name from the accounts. They had been hers to start with, so she felt no guilt about cutting him off. Thankfully, he hadn't wiped out the entire account since the last time she'd checked the balance. Part of her worried that he would. There wasn't much there, but they wouldn't starve. If there was one thing Libbie knew how to do, it was stretch a small amount of food to last several meals.

She left the bank feeling a little better than when she'd walked in. Each action she took seemed to lighten the load. As she drove along Timber Trail, she passed the professional complex where Ethan Townsend's office was located. She made a left turn into the complex and parked at his office. Maybe he knew something that could help her, either with Chris or this perceived curse.

There was no one in the waiting area when she arrived and no receptionist. She stood awkwardly in the middle of the room before deciding to knock on the closed office door. Too late, she realized he might be with a client. Thankfully, when he opened the door, she could see that he was alone. Her breath caught in her throat at the sight of him. She'd already forgotten how attractive he was. He looked every bit as good now as he had during their meeting. He smiled when he saw her.

"Libbie. What a pleasant surprise. How can I help you?"

"I'm so sorry to barge in, but I was passing by and realized I could use your insight. How much do you charge for a consultation?"

"For you, nothing. Come on in." He widened the gap and stepped back so she could enter.

Libbie felt strange being in the office without her friends. The air was charged with an intimacy that hadn't been there during her last visit. Or maybe that was her imagination.

Ethan sat behind the desk and offered a sympathetic smile. "How are you holding up?"

The verbal dam busted open, and Libbie let loose a torrent of words that contained the entirety of events between Inga's death and this moment. Ethan sat quietly and listened. Libbie could tell by the tilt of his head and the kindness in his eyes that he was a good listener and that he cared.

"Wow," he said, once she'd finished. "It's been quite a week for you, Libbie Stark. I'm amazed you're sitting here in one piece. I'd be in the corner curled up in the fetal position and whimpering softly."

She knew a man like him would be doing no such thing, but she appreciated his empathy.

"As far as Chris is concerned, you can take legal action against him," Ethan said.

"It would probably cost me as much in legal fees, though."

Not to mention emotional energy.

"Three mortgage payments, you said? Yeah, you're not wrong."

Libbie appreciated his honesty and that he didn't try to persuade her. "I'm better off handling the missed payments myself and holding it over Chris's head."

Not that she had any leverage. He'd left some belongings at her house, but nothing of any real worth. She'd get more value out of tossing them into the fire pit and burning them than trying to hock them for money.

"Is the house in both your names?" Ethan asked.

"No, it's my house. He moved in after we'd been dating a couple of months. His lease was up, and it just seemed..." She trailed off, wanting to say 'stupid.'

"I understand," Ethan said. "It was convenient and made sense at the time. And then he started handling the bills and it took the burden off you."

Libbie could kick herself. She knew she tended to be too nice and not to make a fuss, but it had never bitten her in the ass quite as badly as this. "My kids and I could've been homeless because I put my trust in the wrong person." They could still be homeless, in fact, if she didn't get her act together and find catering work quickly.

"What about family? Anyone you could ask for an interest-free loan until you're back on your feet?"

Libbie snorted. "No," she said simply.

Although her parents had the money, there was no way she'd ask for it. Chances were good they'd say no, anyway, under the guise of saving it as college tuition for Emily's kids.

"As it happens, I'll be planning a client party at my house soon. If you're interested in catering it, I'd be happy to discuss it with you."

Libbie eyed him closely. "Are you saying that because you've heard my tale of woe?"

"Not at all. I would've considered it either way."

Libbie wasn't sure whether to believe him. "I'm not interested in a handout or a literal pity party."

"It would be neither. In fact, you'd be doing me a huge favor. I should've already planned this, but I've been too busy with client matters to give it attention. I underestimated how much extra work I'd have after Deb died. I feel like I've been digging my way out for months." He gave a rueful shake of his head. "Probably because I have."

Libbie resisted the urge to jump up and do a happy dance. "That sounds great."

"How about coming by Monday night? Unless you already have plans," he added quickly.

"No plans. What time works for you?"

"I'm usually home and out of my suit by seven."

"No need to change on my account." She liked the way he looked in his suit.

He tugged at the knot in his tie. "Trust me. It's the first thing I do when I get home. There are times when I feel imprisoned in my own clothes."

Libbie grew flushed at the thought of liberating him from his...

prison. What was she thinking? Chris was barely out of the house, and this was her lawyer. Okay, not her lawyer exactly, but a potential client at the very least.

"I'll see you on Monday at seven," she said.

She left the office feeling slightly confused by her reaction to him. Nick had just accused her of jumping into a relationship with Chris after their marriage. Now, here she was, fantasizing about the very next man she met. Libbie had never considered herself to be the kind of woman who needed a man in her life, yet her behavior seemed to tell a different story.

Libbie got into her car and chastised herself for being ridiculous. She wasn't dating him. She was meeting him about a job—a job that she desperately needed right now. Their relationship would be strictly professional.

When she crawled into bed later that night and glanced at the empty space beside her, she realized that she didn't feel any sadness at all. Instead, it seemed as though a heavy weight had been lifted from her chest. With Hercules at the base of the bed, acting as her bedroom guardian, Libbie fell asleep to a symphony of crickets and frogs.

# EIGHT

"Your tequila sunrise, just as Inga requested." Kate handed Libbie a tall glass filled to the brim and complete with a little umbrella. The four friends were gathered on Kate's brick patio. Lucas had taken all three kids to the movies so that the women could enjoy their cocktail club time without interference.

"No Prosecco to start?" Libbie asked.

"I thought we'd break from tradition. It seemed appropriate."

"You pulled out all the stops," Libbie said. She shifted the hot pink umbrella to the side for a careful sip.

"And I'm using Inga's tequila," Kate said. "Only the best for our departed friend and, of course, our friend in need."

"Yes, tell us what happened," Julie said from her place at the pale teak table. "Your text was so vague."

That had been deliberate on Libbie's part to avoid having to field different follow-up phone calls. She knew she'd be seeing her friends tonight and preferred to get it all out in one fell swoop. She joined them at the table and shared the down and dirty version.

"Let's find him right now," Julie said, her face flushed with anger and alcohol. "We'll tie him to a tree in the woods, strip off his pants, and coat his balls with honey. He'll either get stung by bees or provide a tasty snack for a bear."

"Quite frankly, I think the bear's too good for him," Kate said.

Libbie nearly spit out her drink as laughter erupted from her throat.

"Do you know where he's staying?" Rebecca asked.

"His friend Brody's," Libbie said. He'd told her that much when he'd finally responded to her angry texts. He'd denied any wrongdoing, of course. Tried to blame Libbie for mishandling funds, but she'd pushed back until he refused to discuss it any further and called her crazy. He then had the gall to ask her to pack the rest of his belongings so he could swing by and collect them another time. She'd agreed but only to be rid of all traces of him, once and for all.

"I know Brody," Rebecca said. "He adopted a dog from the shelter a few months ago. I bet if he knew what Chris did, he'd kick him out."

"I appreciate your support, but I don't need Chris to be homeless just because I might've been," Libbie insisted. "I'll handle this my way."

Kate cocked a thin eyebrow; it was so pale that it was almost transparent against her porcelain skin. "What's your way? Smiling on the outside but crying on the inside?"

Libbie flinched. "No, not this time."

"Why? What's different this time?" Julie pressed.

Libbie raised her chin a fraction. "I am."

"What's your plan?" Rebecca asked. She'd made short work of the tequila sunrise and had switched to water. "How are you going to make the back payments, plus pay your other bills now that you're out of work?"

"I won't be out of work for long. I'll be catering. The overhead is low, and I know where to source the ingredients for less money."

"Who are you, and what have you done with Libbie?" Julie asked with a disbelieving laugh.

Libbie blinked. "What?"

"You sound so...together." Julie seemed to be choosing her words carefully.

"Not that you aren't together," Rebecca added quickly. "You're obviously a great mom, and you were the best thing about Basecamp."

"Joe called me, but I didn't answer," Libbie said.

It had been earlier in the day. She'd let the call go to voicemail and proceeded to listen to Joe beg her to come back. Although she took no pleasure in his pleading tone, she didn't call him back either.

"Good. He doesn't deserve you," Kate said.

Libbie smirked. "According to you, no one seems to deserve me. If that's the case, I might as well book my one-way ticket to a deserted island and shack up with my new best friend, Wilson."

Kate gave a firm shake of her head. "No, that volleyball doesn't deserve you either."

Julie smiled at her. "You said you consulted with that hot lawyer. How was that?"

Libbie tipped back her glass and finished the last of the tequila sunrise. "It was a business meeting. That's how it was."

"Oh, please. I saw the way he looked at you during our meeting," Julie said. "While his mouth was saying legal stuff, his eyes were saying very illegal stuff." She wiggled her eyebrows suggestively.

Libbie's cheeks burned. "What time is the witch due?" She was desperate to change the topic.

"I'm not sure we should call her that," Rebecca said. "What if it's offensive?"

"I don't think it's offensive. If anything, it's aspirational," Kate said. "If Inga was a witch and I aspire to be as awesome as she was..." She shrugged and took a swig of her cocktail.

The doorbell rang, and they froze. Julie was the first to laugh. "Are we scared of her?"

"Her name's Lorraine," Kate said. "How scared can we be?" She scraped back her chair and went to greet their guest.

"What about the ashes?" Rebecca asked. "Are we doing that tonight?"

Libbie shook her head. "Kate's getting them tomorrow, so we'll do it tomorrow night if that works for everyone." They figured maybe the witch would have suggestions, if there was something special they should do with Inga's remains given her true nature. They didn't want to scatter her in the woods without doing some kind of ritual, assuming there was one.

"Will she use the jar Inga left us?" Rebecca asked.

Libbie shrugged. "It was either that or an empty Prosecco bottle. Inga would be fine with either one."

"It isn't as though the ashes are staying there forever," Julie pointed out. "We're scattering them."

Kate returned to the patio, along with an older woman wearing a floor-length kaftan made from a plum-colored jacquard weave. Her gray hair was braided down her back, and she carried a large canvas tote bag that read *I love the person I've become because I fought to become her*.

"This looks like a fun party." The older woman smiled at them. "I'm Lorraine, Soul Seer or Messenger of the Spirits. I can't decide which one I like better."

"I thought you were the Voice of the Moon Goddess," Kate said.

"Not anymore," Lorraine said. "It didn't suit me after a couple years."

"I like Soul Seer," Rebecca said. "Then again, I'm a sucker for alliteration."

"Would you like a drink?" Kate offered. "We have a full bar."

Lorraine's face flashed with recognition. "Ah, right. This is the cocktail club." She glanced over her shoulder toward the teak bar that matched the rest of the patio set. "I wouldn't object to a dirty martini."

"I can handle that one. It's my husband's favorite." Kate retreated behind the bar to fix the cocktail.

Lorraine moved in a half circle, drinking in each woman as she went. "I understand you ladies need information."

Libbie looked her straight in the eye. "That's right. We've

recently learned about witches, and we'd like to know more. As much wisdom as you can impart."

"I see," Lorraine said slowly. "And how did you happen to hear about witches, if you don't mind me asking?"

"We've inherited some assets," Libbie said, gauging Lorraine's reaction to her use of the word 'assets.' "We're a little confused and thought you could help."

Lorraine dropped the tote bag onto the patio with a thud. "You mean you're witches, too."

"I'm not sure that we need to slap a label on it," Kate said. She returned to the table and passed the martini glass to their guest.

Lorraine tipped her head back and gave a throaty laugh. "It's not a label, honey. It's an honor. Embrace it."

Libbie stared into her glass as she digested the words. "We're really witches," she said, more to herself.

"Not what you pictured, are we?" Lorraine asked. "You wanted a wart on my nose. Trust me, I have a wart. It just isn't anywhere visible, thank Goddess." She sipped her martini and sighed. "Wonderful work, darling. You're a natural."

Libbie chewed her lip, debating her next question. "What if I don't want it?"

Lorraine regarded her. "Don't want what?"

"To be a witch. What if I want to go back to being me?"

Lorraine pinned her with a hard look. "Were you really you in the first place?"

Libbie didn't know how to respond. "I feel like I've been cursed."

"Ask yourself why that is." Lorraine took Kate's empty chair and settled beside Libbie.

"That's easy. Ever since we opened Pandora's box of bad breath, things have started to go wrong. I quit my job. My boyfriend left me and took my money with him." Libbie rubbed her temples. "My life is a mess."

Lorraine fixed her with a penetrating stare. "Is it actually a mess, darling, or are you simply uncomfortable with being uncomfortable?"

"I'm not going to be able to pay my bills, so I guess I'm uncomfortable with the idea of my kids and me being homeless."

Seemed reasonable to Libbie.

"You're a messenger to the spirit world," Julie said. "Can we get in touch with our friend? The one who left us her gifts? Maybe she could explain how this works and if Libbie really doesn't want to keep hers..."

"Libbie is keeping hers," Kate interjected. "I know things seem bleak right now, but I think you're headed in the right direction. And if you take time to reflect on it, I think you'll agree with me."

Lorraine's brow creased. "If your friend was truly a witch, I'm not so sure I can reach her. Witches don't usually hang around afterward. They have better places to be. It's basically the way I feel every time my cousin Marta has a LuLaRoe party. I could tie my leggings together and rappel down Mount Everest. That's how many I've collected."

Libbie felt conflicted. On the one hand, it seemed as though Godzilla himself had marched straight through her life, breathing fire as he went. On the other hand, she felt...better.

"Can we at least try?" Libbie asked. As much as anything, she was curious to see how Lorraine went about contacting spirits, and it would be helpful to understand more about these so-called gifts.

Lorraine's gaze swept around the table. "For what it's worth, my advice is to simply surrender. Instead of resisting, listen to what the universe is trying to teach you."

"I like that idea," Kate said.

"Only because you're not the one being bitch-slapped by the universe right now," Libbie shot back. She shifted her focus to Lorraine. "Full steam ahead, please."

"Mind if I toke up? Smoking brings me clarity."

Libbie noticed Kate stiffen; her friend was averse to smoke of any kind.

Kate glanced around at the furniture. "Just move those other cushions to the edge of the patio. I don't want the smell getting into them. They're dry clean only."

"Who has outdoor cushions that are dry clean only?" Lorraine asked.

While Julie and Rebecca moved the cushions, Lorraine removed several items from her tote bag, including a tall white candle, a pre-rolled joint, and a folded square of fabric. She unfolded the fabric and covered the teak table with—

"Is that Hello Kitty?" Libbie asked, squinting at the images on the tablecloth.

"Don't you love her?" Lorraine asked.

Courtney had gone through an incredibly brief Hello Kitty phase, and Libbie had been relieved when it passed quickly. She didn't see the appeal.

The women sat around the smiling faces of Hello Kitty as Lorraine prepared for her seance. She lit the candle and then the joint. "That's the good stuff."

Kate replenished everyone's drinks while Lorraine smoked her joint.

"The downside is these burn too fast," Lorraine said. "I'll save the rest for later." She placed the remaining joint on a small ceramic plate that Kate had placed in front of her. Libbie was pretty sure it was intended to hold Kate's rings when she was in the kitchen cooking.

"The smell is a bit nauseating," Kate said.

Julie sniffed the air, as though she needed to confirm. "There's a nice breeze tonight. That will help."

"Please place your hands on the table," Lorraine instructed. "Your drinks will have to wait."

"We don't hold hands?" Kate asked.

Lorraine leveled her with a look. "Did I say hold hands?"

Kate placed her fingers primly on the edge of the table.

Lorraine closed her eyes. "Now close your eyes and repeat after me."

They repeated Lorraine's Latin phrases. They didn't exactly roll off the tongue, and Libbie heard herself tripping over some of the words. Libbie was relieved when the witch finally switched to English.

"We call forth Inga." Lorraine popped open an eye. "What's her last name?"

"Paulsen," Libbie said.

She closed her eye. "We call forth Inga Paulsen. Inga, your sisters are here to greet you and thank you for their gifts."

Libbie watched the flame of the candle flicker. There was no sign of Inga's spirit or any other.

Lorraine tried again. "Are you there, Inga Paulsen? It's me, Lorraine." She chuckled. "That one's for the Judy Blume fans."

Libbie snorted.

"Will the spirits come if the seer is cracking jokes and not taking communication seriously?" Kate asked.

Lorraine rolled her eyes. "Relax, kitten. The spirits have a sense of humor, just like when they were people." She looped her shoulders and tried again. "We beseech you, Inga Paulsen. Come forth and impart your wisdom unto your sisters."

At that moment, Cat-Cat jumped onto the table and purred, prompting a scream from Julie. Libbie bit the inside of her cheek to keep from laughing.

"This cat belonged to your friend," Lorraine said.

"How did you know?" Kate asked.

"Her tag. It says *If lost, please return to Inga P.*" Lorraine's laughter quickly morphed into a cough. "Sorry, I couldn't resist. I could tell by looking at her. I sense a connection."

Libbie frowned at the cat. Would she sense a connection when she looked at Cat-Cat or Eliza? She hadn't really focused much on the cat, other than to make sure Eliza and Hercules got along.

"I'd like to ask Inga if there's any special ritual we're supposed to do when we scatter her ashes," Rebecca said.

Lorraine looked at her. "I can answer that one. The answer is do whatever you feel honors your friend. If that's a spiritual ritual, then do it. If that's spreading her ashes at the base of a tree while quoting your favorite one-liners from The Golden Girls, that's fine too."

Kate pursed her lips. "So this means no Inga?"

"I think this cat is the closest we're going to get. Sorry, ladies. Anyone else you want me to try?" Lorraine asked.

Libbie slumped against her chair. "Inga is the only one with answers."

Cat-Cat meowed, and Kate lifted her off the table and set her on the patio.

"What are your specific questions?" Lorraine asked. "Maybe I can help."

Libbie didn't wait for anyone else to ask. She jumped right in with hers. "Why didn't she tell us what the gifts are? She left everything so vague. Even her letter told us to open the jar and nothing else. 'Breath is the spirit' isn't exactly chock full of details."

Lorraine's eyes appeared bloodshot in the candlelight. "She couldn't tell you because she didn't know. She might've had a guess, but there's no way to know for sure until after the assets have been passed on and, by that time, the original witch is too dead to see the outcome."

"Then how are we supposed to know if we're witches?" Julie asked. "Except for the moment when we opened the jar, I don't feel any different."

"Me, either," Kate said.

"Same," Rebecca added.

"If you inherited her assets, then you're witches," Lorraine said. "It's that simple."

Libbie closed her eyes, trying to understand. "If Inga had a magical cocktail book like mine, then why did she have bartenders at our weekly club? We never had any unusual drinks without names."

Lorraine squinted at her. "What makes you think Inga could

do everything you can do? You're Elizabeth Stark, not Inga Paulsen. You have different experiences and personal history. The magic gives you what you need. It's impossible to know how it will manifest. It's unique just like the individual person." She smiled. "Like you, Libbie."

"Okay, then why am I the only one experiencing changes, if she divided her assets among us?" Libbie asked. "And why am I the only one with writing in the book she left me? Granted, it was only one recipe, but the others don't have writing in theirs."

Lorraine eyed them one at a time, her gaze finally coming to rest on Libbie. "You were the only one ready to receive your gifts." She waved a hand in the direction of the others. "These ladies, not so much."

Kate folded her arms. "I beg your pardon. I can assure you that we are every bit as ready to receive whatever Inga left for us. We loved that woman like she was our own flesh and blood."

"Even more than our own flesh and blood," Libbie added. "I would've traded my mother for Inga in a heartbeat." She gasped at her own words. "I didn't mean that."

Lorraine's upper lip curled. "Sure you did, kitten. No judgment here. We all have our crosses to bear." She shifted to address the other women. "When the gifts are ready to be received, they make themselves known. Like I said before, surrender, and listen to what the universe is trying to teach you."

"How do we convince the universe we're ready to receive our gift?" Julie asked. "Is there a text alert we can send?"

"Nope." Lorraine blew out the candle, and a blanket of darkness fell over them. "There's no convincing. You're not in front of a jury box. You just have to be patient."

"What about Libbie?" Julie asked. "How can she make things right? She lost her job, her boyfriend."

"Sometimes we have to shed our skin in order to reveal what was already underneath," Lorraine said. "How old are you, Libbie?"

"Forty-eight."

Lorraine nodded. "Yes. This is your time."

"Midlife is my time?" she echoed. "I don't think so. Midlife is when I start discovering that my body isn't keeping up with my mind and my mind isn't keeping up with my heart." She paused. "The symbolic heart, not the organ. I guess, technically, that's part of the body."

Julie laughed. "Someone pour her another drink."

"Holy Hemsworth, I've got it," Julie said.

"Which one?" Lorraine asked.

"Any one of them will do, but Chris is my preference," Julie said. She turned toward Libbie. "How can you make this situation the best thing that ever happened to you?"

Kate gave Julie's arm a light smack. "That's a great question."

Julie rubbed her arm. "Then why are you hitting me?"

"Because I should've thought of it."

Libbie's mind drew a blank. "I have no idea."

"That's where I'd start," Lorraine said. "Figure out the answer, and you'll be well on your way."

"I guess this why Ethan Townsend didn't have a lot of information for us," Libbie said. "Each case is too specific."

"Ethan Townsend?" Lorraine repeated. "I know that name."

"Yes, he's the lawyer who consulted with you about the whole witch thing," Libbie told her. "So he could better understand Inga's will."

"Oh, Ethan didn't come to me about witchcraft. That discovery was a happy accident, or as I like to call it, divine intervention. He came to me because he wanted to see if I could summon his sister. We ended up chatting, and that's how he learned I was a witch. I only advertise myself as a psychic, you see. That's what clients are interested in."

"And did you?" Libbie pressed. "Contact his sister?"

Lorraine patted her hand. "That's confidential, doll. Just like a lawyer, I have standards, and I adhere to them."

Fair enough.

"If you have no other questions, I'll be going." Lorraine gathered her belongings, and the women lifted their glasses so she could retrieve her tablecloth.

"Thank you for coming," Libbie said.

Lorraine slung her bag over her shoulder. "I'm sorry about your friend, but I always see a witch's passing as a blessing. It means the torch has been passed once again." She smiled at them. "I can't see the future, but I sense you'll make very fine witches. Welcome to the sisterhood."

"I'll walk you out." As Kate stood to escort her to the door, Lorraine stopped her.

"I'll show myself out. You stay here with your friends. Enjoy this wonderful evening."

They waited until she was out of earshot to speak.

"Do you think she was a real witch?" Julie asked.

"She had to be. Did you notice her chin? It had more hairs than Lenny Jenkins' back. And we all know his mother Nairs his for him." Libbie clamped a hand over her mouth. Had those words actually come from her own mouth?

Julie laughed. "I think you inhaled some of her weed."

"How could she not? It was so strong." Kate wrinkled her nose.

Rebecca rubbed her own chin thoughtfully. "I don't think chin hair is any indication of a witch. If that were true, every menopausal woman in the world would qualify."

"Forget witches. If it weren't for those wax strips I buy on Amazon, I'd look like I was shifting into a werewolf," Julie said.

They sat in silence for a moment, contemplating what they'd learned.

"Are you feeling any better about everything?" Julie asked.

Libbie heaved a sigh. "Maybe? I don't know. I'd feel a lot better if I knew my catering business would be successful."

Kate snapped her fingers. "Mrs. Quincy."

Libbie conjured an image of the intimidating woman who owned a small salon chain. Her husband's family had lived in town since its inception and, as his wife, she held a lot of sway with the other residents. "What about her?"

"What's her big to-do every year?" Kate prompted.

Libbie fell back against her chair, the realization hitting her. "Her Labor Day party."

"Every influential person in town attends that party," Kate said. "If you can convince her to let you cater it, you'll be turning business away by the end of the year because you'll be so in demand."

"Kate's right," Julie chimed in. "Mrs. Quincy's blessing is basically a heap of money in the bank. You'll be able to pay the mortgage company in a lump sum. You won't even need a repayment plan."

Libbie doubted it would be that much of a windfall. "Doesn't she usually hire Pedro?" Libbie asked. Pedro Montague was the owner and chef of a popular local restaurant.

Kate smiled. "I was at the salon the other day, and Mrs. Quincy was complaining to anyone who would listen that Pedro can't do it this year because he'll be on his honeymoon. He and Cyrus are touring southeast Asia. So she was asking for recommendations."

Libbie felt a fire light in her belly at the thought of winning over Mrs. Quincy. Her friends were right. If she managed to impress Mrs. Quincy and her guests, it would kickstart her business in a way no amount of marketing could replicate. She'd be sure to make her repayments, and then some.

"Thanks. That's a great idea. I'll speak to her tomorrow," Libbie said.

"Won't you need a few days to practice what you want to say?" Julie asked.

"No, I'm good."

The other women exchanged baffled glances. "Just like that?" Kate asked. "No excuses as to why you're not ready or not talented enough?"

"I'm channeling Inga," Libbie said. "How can I make upending my life the best thing that ever happened to me? I can start by paying a visit to Mrs. Quincy."

"Tomorrow's Saturday, so she'll be at the salon here in Cloverleaf," Kate said. "Let me know if you want me to make a call."

Libbie knew deep in her bones this was something she had to do on her own. "Thanks, Kate. I appreciate the offer, but I've got this."

NINE

Libbie pushed open the door to the salon and walked straight up to the reception desk like a woman on a mission—a mission that involved crab puffs and parmesan tomato chips. "Good morning, Lacey. Is Mrs. Quincy available, by any chance?"

"Hi. Are you on the schedule today?" Lacey asked.

Libbie could tell the young woman was trying to remember her name. "No, I'm not here for my hair. I just need a quick moment of her time. It's about her Labor Day party."

The young woman angled her head. "She's in the back office. You can go ahead."

Libbie offered a relieved smile. "Thanks."

She hurried through the busy salon and kept her eyes focused on the office in case there was someone there she knew. She wasn't in the mood for chitchat. Truth be told, Libbie was never in the mood for idle chitchat. Her close friends were her comfort level, and anything else left her exhausted for hours afterward.

Mrs. Quincy sat behind an antique desk repainted in bubblegum pink. As Libbie entered the room, a beagle shot forward to sniff her feet. She hadn't even noticed Trixie was there until the dog moved. She bent over to pet the dog, unable to resist a four-legged friend.

"Good morning," Mrs. Quincy said. "How can I help you?"

"Good morning, Mrs. Quincy. I hope you don't mind me dropping by unexpectedly, but I understand Pedro's unable to cater your Labor Day party this year, and I'd like to throw my hat in the ring."

She produced one of the flyers from her handbag and set it on the desk, taking a quick second to admire her daughter's artistic handiwork.

Mrs. Quincy read the name on the flyer out loud. "Libbie Stark." She met Libbie's anxious gaze. "I know your mother and sister, don't I? They're regular customers."

"So am I," Libbie said, more meekly than she would've liked.

"I cater to your whole family, and now you want to cater for me." Mrs. Quincy looked her over. "Have a seat, Ms. Stark."

Libbie lowered herself onto the upholstered chair, and Trixie's front paws appeared beside her. Someone wasn't through with her need for affection yet. She resumed petting the dog while they talked.

"You have catering experience?"

"Not yet, but I've been a chef for many years. I worked at Basecamp until recently."

Mrs. Quincy nodded. "Good food but uninspired. I hope you don't intend to serve my guests meatloaf kebabs."

Libbie laughed. "If I never cook another meatloaf, it will be too soon."

"Well, you have experience cooking for large groups. That's a definite plus. My Labor Day party tends to get out of hand when it comes to the guest list. I hate to say no."

Libbie wanted to make certain that one day in the near future, Mrs. Quincy would hate to say no to *her*. "I took the liberty of creating menu options." She produced another laminated sheet from her bag that described the dishes in greater detail and included Courtney's depictions of the food.

"Well, now I'm hungry, so thank you for that." Mrs. Quincy set the paper on the desk and smiled. "I appreciate you coming to see me. I like a woman with moxie, reminds me of myself, but I can't hire someone without catering experience. As I'm sure you're aware, this party is the social event of the season. I feel about this the way I feel about drugstore hair dye. I can't take the risk."

Libbie tried to disguise her disappointment. Did she really think it would be that easy? When had anything in her life ever been easy? "Mrs. Quincy, I know I can do this. I'm organized. I'm an excellent chef. I know what people like, which dishes will spark their interest."

"I'm sure you do."

"I'd even be willing to set up a tasting, if you like. I'll make a few of your preferred options or, if you have something you'd like me to make—a Labor Day staple, for example—I'm happy to do that, too."

Libbie was surprised by the sense of calm that surrounded her. She expected anxiety to be burning a hole in her stomach right now.

Trixie tapped Libbie's arm to encourage more petting. Libbie smiled and scratched the beagle behind the ear.

Mrs. Quincy eyed her closely. "I'll tell you what, Trixie seems to like you, and that's not to be ignored. I interviewed a caterer yesterday, and I was afraid Trixie would take a bite out of his butt before he left. If the dog snarls or growls, that's a hard pass from me."

Libbie would've kissed the dog on the lips if it wouldn't have seemed too awkward. "I have a dog. And a cat."

"Oh? What kind?"

"Hercules is an Irish Setter, and Eliza is...adopted from a friend who passed away."

Mrs. Quincy's expression softened. "I'm sorry to hear that, but glad to hear that you were able to take her in." She rapped her cotton candy-colored fingernails on the desk. "Here's the deal, Ms. Stark. If you can successfully cater three local events in the next month—nothing too small, mind you, I'll let you cater my party."

Libbie remained planted in the chair, despite her desire to

launch herself across the table and hug Mrs. Quincy. "Thank you. You won't regret it." She paused. "How will you know whether I've actually been successful?"

"References, darling. No family members, of course. You'll provide me with the menus you prepared and three glowing references, and the party is yours."

"Not that I'm concerned, but what if you don't hire me for some reason? Will you be able to find someone good that close to the date?" Libbie silently cursed herself for the question; it reeked of self-doubt.

"I have a plan B, but she catered Lila Kensington's Memorial Day party, and I don't like to appear to follow in Lila's footsteps, if you understand what I mean."

Libbie's head bobbed up and down so fast she was afraid her head would snap off. "Thank you so much, Mrs. Quincy. I really appreciate the opportunity." She bent down and kissed the top of Trixie's head before rising to a standing position.

"Good luck, Ms. Stark. Be sure to keep me updated."

Libbie felt like flying out of the salon, but she forced herself to take slow, steady steps across the linoleum. She hadn't felt excitement like this in such a long time. All at once, the world seemed hopeful and full of possibilities. She couldn't wait to share the good news with her friends.


"I need to cater three jobs, and I need to do them well enough to get glowing references, and then she'll hire me," Libbie said.

She and Julie sat on the deck of the sprawling house that Julie shared with her mother. They each had a glass of iced tea and a frosted strawberry Pop-Tart, one of Julie's weaknesses. The unobstructed view of the island in the middle of the lake made this one of Libbie's favorite spots in town.

It helped that her good friend lived here.

"That's encouraging," Julie said. "I'm so proud of you, waltzing into the salon like that. You're a culinary badass."

"Thanks. It still feels a little surreal." The old Libbie would've called and prayed that Mrs. Quincy was unavailable so she could leave an awkward voicemail.

"Any idea who else is in need of a caterer this summer?" Julie asked.

"Not yet, but I'm on it. I've been distributing flyers and Josh is putting some up at the club. Nick has them at Cone Hut too."

"That's nice of him."

"I thought so, too."

Julie smiled. "It isn't like Nick to be thoughtful. I wonder if Olivia made him do it."

Nick's wife seemed to be a positive influence on Libbie's ex, so Libbie made sure to stay on her good side. "I wondered that myself. Either way, I'm grateful." Her head tilted back. "How's Der Kommissar?"

Julie huffed. "Don't ask. She has an ingrown toenail and seems to think it's my familial duty to take care of it."

Libbie shuddered. "Makes me glad I'm not close with my parents. They'll expect Emily to do that stuff, I guess."

"Oh, please, Cinderella. They'll expect you to do the gross stuff while they prep Emily for the ball. They wouldn't want their precious younger child to get her hands dirty."

Libbie suspected her friend was right. Her parents had placed unreasonable expectations on Libbie for as long as she could remember and vilified her whenever she dared to push back, which was rare thanks to Libbie's aversion to conflict.

"Julie? Do you have company?" Doris appeared at the screen door and peered at them on the deck. She wore a peach-colored robe and slippers and leaned on a cane.

"Mom, what are you doing down here? You know you're not supposed to take the stairs."

Doris pushed aside the screen door and joined them on the deck. "Oh, it's only Libbie. I thought maybe you were entertaining a male visitor."

"Why would I do that? You know I'm not interested in dating."

Doris hobbled over to the table and plucked Julie's glass of iced tea from the table. "Does this have sugar?"

"No, just lemon." Julie's expression was as sour as the aforementioned fruit as her mother brought the glass to her mouth and drank a generous mouthful.

"Maybe you could consider bringing your mother a drink. I'm dying of thirst up there, sequestered in my tower. It's like a Rapunzel reversal, where the poor mother is imprisoned instead."

Julie's jaw unhinged. "Mom, I brought you a cup of tea less than an hour ago."

"Tea is dehydrating. You should have brought me hot water with a squeeze of lemon. On second thought, you'll overdo it. Just set the lemon wedge on the saucer, and I'll do it myself."

Libbie turned her gaze to the dozen or so boats and kayaks on the rippling water. She hated being present for Julie and her mother's squabbles. Greg had served as a barrier between them up until his death. Now Doris was free to harass Julie to her heart's content and took full advantage of the opportunity.

"Why don't you go back upstairs, and I'll bring you hot water in a few minutes?" Julie asked.

"Fine, but I'm timing you," Doris said. "Too long and you're fired."

"You can't fire me. I'm your daughter."

"I can write you out of the will. There's still time."

Julie rolled her eyes. She'd clearly heard this one before. "And leave it to whom? Brad?"

"He is your brother," Doris sniffed.

Libbie vaguely remembered Julie's older brother, Brad. He'd moved to Phoenix more than twenty years ago and rarely called or visited. The last time he'd returned to Lake Cloverleaf was for their father's funeral. He hadn't even made the trip when Greg died, citing a scheduling conflict. Julie had tried to appear nonchalant at the time, but Libbie knew it had to hurt.

"Libbie is setting up a catering business," Julie said in what

Libbie recognized as a desperate effort to change the subject. "Isn't that great?"

Doris assessed Libbie. "What happened with Joe? I bet he tried to grab your ass, and you acted like it was a case of assault and battery." She clucked her tongue in disapproval. "Women today are so soft."

Julie sucked in a breath, and Libbie knew her friend was trying very hard to be on her best behavior. "Libbie's in the running to cater Mrs. Quincy's Labor Day party, but she has to cater three other events first."

Doris leaned on her cane. "Is that so? Well, you should talk to Myra Kitts' daughter-in-law."

"Serena?" Julie queried.

"Yes. She's planning a fancy barbecue because her husband got a big promotion. Myra says he's rolling in dough now."

"Thanks for the tip," Libbie said. It sounded like exactly the kind of affair that would impress Mrs. Quincy if she handled it right.

"See? Old people don't need to be put out to pasture. We still have our uses." Slowly, Doris rotated back toward the kitchen and disappeared from view. Libbie could her the faint click of her cane as she crossed the tile floor.

Julie lowered her voice. "I don't care that she's old. I care that she's a complete bitch."

"Have you considered moving her bedroom downstairs?" Libbie asked. "The house has plenty of rooms on the main level that could be turned into a bedroom."

"I've made the suggestion, but you know Doris. She refuses to budge. She'll probably call the police if I try to relocate her downstairs."

Libbie didn't envy Julie. "I wish she appreciated you more."

Julie wrapped her fingers around her glass. "It's just how she is. She'll never change."

"No, I'm sure you're right."

Julie managed a smile. "Hey, at least you've got a lead on a job now. It was worth tolerating her for five minutes."

"How is she plugged in to the town gossip from her bedroom?"

"Because she's plugged in to the internet. She and her friends have a private chat room, and once a week they play cards via video chat. You know it's in progress because Mom ends up shouting 'cheater' at least once per session. The first time it happened, I thought she was watching an old Jerry Springer."

"I guess that's good for you. Keeps her occupied."

"Not occupied enough." Julie heaved a sigh. "I feel awful saying anything. She's my mother."

Libbie patted her friend's hand on the table. "You're preaching to the converted, Jules."

"I know, right? Between the two of us, we'd keep a therapist busy for the rest of her career."

"I thought about asking my mother if she'd go to therapy sessions with me. Nick had suggested it, actually, back when we were married, but I knew what her reaction would be. In her mind, she does nothing wrong, and I'm the problem. Her difficult child."

"You're only difficult when you won't do exactly as she wants when she wants. She's like my mom. She wants everything on her terms."

Libbie nodded absently. Her mind was on Mrs. Quincy's challenge and how easily she could track down Serena Kitts. "Do you know where the Kitts live?"

"They're on the north side of the lake, but Serena will probably be at the lakefront bar with her friends at lunchtime."

"Liquid lunch?"

Julie ate the last bite of her Pop-Tart. "They take their cocktails even more seriously than we do."

"Which bar?"

"Pebbles. You can't miss her. Tall, willowy brunette with flawless skin. She's always dressed like she's headed to a New York fashion show."

"Thanks, I'll head over there now and lie in wait."

Julie looked at her in surprise. "Are you really going over there? I thought for sure you'd decide to wait for her to go home. She'll be with the other Ladies Who Lunch."

"That's okay. I can handle it."

Julie eyed her suspiciously. "Next time I see you, bring me a copy of that cocktail recipe in Inga's book. I might want to make one for myself."

Libbie laughed. "I don't think rum stays in the system this long, but sure. I'll show it to you."

"I don't think it was the rum, Lib."

Libbie ran a finger along the side of her glass. "What do you mean?"

"I mean I think there might've been something really special about that cocktail."

"The fern?"

Julie gazed at her in wonder. "No, Libbie. I think it was magic."

# TEN

Pebbles was the lakefront bar that catered to the middle-aged crowd. After ten in the evening, it became a haven for divorced people seeking their next date, which Libbie inadvertently discovered after she and Nick split up. For that reason alone, she'd formed the habit of avoiding the place. Everyone there seemed to reek of desperation. Even now, in the middle of the day, the patrons seemed to reek of more than alcohol.

As Julie promised, Serena Kitt was easy to spot. She wore a wide-brimmed hat and enormous black sunglasses. Her skin was lightly bronzed from the sun. She smiled, revealing a set of the whitest, straightest teeth Libbie had ever seen. She sat at a four-top with two other women, and Libbie recognized the fair redhead as Peyton Lansing. Peyton had been two years younger than Libbie in high school but seemed to attend every senior event from her freshmen year onward. The other woman looked familiar, but Libbie didn't know her name. Her reddish-brown hair was in twists, and her fawn skin appeared to have burned and freckled thanks to the intensity of the summer sun.

Libbie approached the table with a friendly smile plastered across her face. "Serena?"

The woman lowered her sunglasses and looked at Libbie. "Yes?"

"Hi, I'm so sorry to interrupt. My name's Libbie Stark. I understand you're in the market for a caterer and, as it happens, I've just launched my business, so I thought I'd pass along my information, if you're interested."

Serena scrutinized her for a silent moment, and Libbie worried that she'd overstepped. "Join us, Libbie Stark." She pushed out the empty chair with her sandaled foot. "I'd love to hear more about your business."

Libbie slid into the chair and pulled out her marketing materials. "This is for your husband's promotion, right?"

Peyton's eyes widened as she read the menu options. "Crab puffs are my favorite. You have to have those, Serena."

Libbie placed the packet in the middle of the table for the women to ogle.

Serena smiled at her other friend. "I even see vegetarian options for you, Ally."

"I can work within your budget," Libbie said. "I just need to know the number of guests, whether we'll use disposables or china and glassware, and the style of the event."

Serena stopped her with a look. "You're hired."

Libbie heard a sharp intake of breath and realized it came from her. "I am?"

"As long as our schedules are compatible, yes."

Ally snorted. "She's easily convinced after a couple of cocktails."

"It has nothing to do with alcohol," Serena said. "I've been needing to make a decision about this and haven't gotten around to it."

Peyton laughed. "Because you're too busy having drinks with your friends?"

Serena ignored her and cut a glance at Libbie. "Why don't we discuss this in more detail at my house? Are you free now?"

"Are you sure? I don't mean to drag you away." Libbie shot a guilty look at her two companions.

"These two want to ogle the bartender, but I don't care for excessive man chest."

"Prude," Ally said, smiling.

Serena stood. "I'll see you bitches later."

"TTFN," Peyton said, and blew her a kiss.

"Can I offer you a ride home?" Libbie asked, as they walked away from the table.

Serena waved a dismissive hand. "Oh, no. We take the jitney so no one has to drive." She glanced over her shoulder. "Peyton, what time is the next jitney?"

"Not for another hour," Peyton called back.

Serena turned back toward Libbie. "I suppose I'll take you up on that ride, after all."

At least they were responsible. "No problem." Libbie steered Serena to the parking lot, keeping one hand within reach of the slightly inebriated woman in case she toppled over.

Once they were settled in the car, Serena looked at her. "I'm so glad you sought me out. I've been putting this off, and it's going to bite me in the ass if I don't get everything sorted quickly."

"Any particular reason you've put it off?"

Serena's gaze drifted to the passenger-side window. "The weight of expectation, I suppose. My husband has gotten this big promotion, and he likes things a certain way, but he doesn't like to actually make the plans himself. It becomes a guessing game, where I hope I guess right." She pointed. "You'll want to make the next right."

"What happens if you guess wrong?"

"Sulking, normally. I hate sulking, don't you? It's so childlike. I blame his mother."

Libbie laughed. "Why do we never blame their fathers? Surely they also have a responsibility to teach their children to communicate rather than sulk."

"I couldn't agree more. Sadly, my husband is far too busy with a death grip on the corporate ladder to teach his son anything." Serena didn't even try to hide her bitterness.

"How old is your son?"

"Caeden's fifteen and proving to be a real challenge at the moment."

"Oh, my son Josh is sixteen. They might know each other from school."

"It's possible. Caeden doesn't talk much about his friends." Her laugh rang hollow. "The truth is, Caeden doesn't talk about much of anything these days. If he grunts in my direction, I find myself jumping for joy." She tapped the dashboard. "Right here, hon." She laughed again. "Pardon my manners. What's your name again? I've already forgotten."

"Libbie Stark." She pulled into the semi-circular driveway of a house with cedar shake siding painted a dark gray. Three front steps made of dark concrete slabs led to a white-trimmed covered porch with an arched ceiling. Libbie thought the exterior was stunning without feeling too fussy.

"Come on in, Libbie Stark, and we'll talk business." Serena seemed sharper as they approached the front door. Maybe the afternoon alcohol was wearing off.

"Is Caeden working this summer?"

She barked a laugh as she unlocked the front door. "I wish." She glanced at Libbie with renewed interest. "Your son has a job?"

"He's a lifeguard at Club Cloverleaf."

Serena tilted her head back and groaned. "I would love for Caeden to do something like that. He's an excellent swimmer." She sauntered through the expansive foyer with its sweeping staircase and into the coastal-style kitchen. Libbie marveled at the driftwood-finished flooring and the tongue-and-groove planks on the ceiling. Six burners. European convection oven. Serena's kitchen would be a dream for someone like Libbie.

"Let me show you some menu options." Libbie didn't want to waste time digging through her bag, so she pulled out the entire contents and set them on the counter.

"How do you do it?" Serena asked as she opened the refrigerator and poked her head inside.

"It's not hard. I choose a selection of complementary dishes and—"

Serena spun around. "No, not that. Your son. How do you raise a responsible son who has a job and"—she waved a hand—"speaks to you?"

Libbie hesitated, uncertain how to answer the question. She didn't think she'd done anything special with her kids. They seemed to be great without too much effort from her.

"Caeden doesn't talk to you?"

"I told you. He grunts. I'm pretty sure he's lying to me whenever he does deign to speak to me."

"Have you tried asking him?"

Serena twisted the lid off a bottle of sparkling water. "To be perfectly honest, I think I'm afraid. What if he tells me something I don't want to know? What if too much talk reveals he's a horrible teenager? Then I only have myself to blame."

"I don't think this is a situation where ignorance is bliss. I know he's fifteen, but he's still young enough to need his mother's guidance."

Serena's cheeks were tinged with pink. "What's wrong with me? I shouldn't be unloading my tales of parental woe on you. It's unprofessional."

Libbie offered a sympathetic smile. "No judgment here. We all our have our struggles." She sifted through the contents to find the sample menu, feeling flustered at the thought of appearing disorganized. Her hand brushed over the top of Inga's book, and the pages flipped open. Libbie froze at the sight of an unfamiliar cocktail recipe—a recipe that definitely hadn't been there the last time she'd looked.

"Is something wrong?" Serena asked. She moved to stand beside Libbie and glanced at the open book. "Ooh, that looks delicious."

Libbie stared at the image of the pale pink cocktail with its curled rhubarb garnish.

Serena tapped the page. "This is exactly the kind of cocktail we need for the party. Something different that the guests won't be tired of. Why don't you make it for me? I should probably do a taste test, don't you think?" She winked. "I'll pour us water for now. I'm sure I can use a little rehydration."

"You want to make this?" Libbie asked. Her pulse sped up as she contemplated what to do. She was a chef, not a bartender. Besides, she had no idea what the effects of the cocktail would be. What if it harmed Serena? "Wouldn't you rather see the food menu?"

Serena seemed intent on the cocktail. "As I'm sure you can guess, I have an extensive liquor cabinet." She inclined her head toward the page. "I even have fennel."

"You do?"

"Of course. Everybody knows it's the new celery."

Libbie could tell she wouldn't be able to dissuade Serena, and she really needed to book the party. "I'll need to infuse the vermouth with the fennel. That takes a few days because it needs to chill in the refrigerator."

"Looks like it will be worth the wait. Why don't you get started? We can discuss the menu while you work your magic."

Libbie's heart skipped a beat at the mention of magic, and she laughed awkwardly. "I'll do my best." She cleared her throat, trying to harness her newfound confidence. "Right now, I'll need a glass container, vermouth, a sieve, rhubarb, and fennel. Oh, and a blender."

"No problem. My kitchen is your kitchen."

While Serena retrieved the necessary items, Libbie located the sample menu and placed it on the counter. She couldn't believe she was actually going through with this. What if the cocktail for Serena upended the woman's life like the one Libbie made for herself that upended hers? Then again, maybe Serena Kitts' life needed a bit of upending. She'd already hinted at issues in the brief time Libbie had known her.

Serena sat on a stool at the island while Libbie set to work. She tried to maintain her air of confidence as she followed the first part of the instructions. Despite her regular attendance at the cocktail club meetings, she didn't consider herself a mixologist. She had a passing interest in some of the more complicated cocktails they'd made over the years, but she'd never even tried to make one for herself at home. The thought hadn't occurred to her until the night she'd made the recipe from the book.

"Libbie, I have to say, I love your creative spirit," Serena said, scanning the information. "I'm a big fan of food as an art form."

"So am I. I just didn't get to exercise that muscle at my old job, which is why I quit. Chicken parm with five cheeses was the most adventurous thing on the menu."

Serena laughed. "Oh, the horror. Well, if it's any consolation, I think you made the right decision. Easy for me to say, though, right? I'm not the one who has to pay your bills."

The more time Libbie spent with Serena Kitts, the more she liked her. Her first instinct had been to be wary. Women with meticulous appearances and money to burn reminded her too much of her mother, and she tended to steer clear. Arguably, Kate fit that bill, but Libbie and Kate had been friends long before Kate was a YouTube sensation, and the same rules didn't apply.

They chatted about the menu options and the number of guests. It wouldn't be a large crowd, for which Libbie was grateful. Thirty to forty people would be enough to satisfy Mrs. Quincy. Libbie needed to get her bearings as a caterer, and this seemed like the ideal way to do it. Serena seemed torn between a few of the appetizers, and Libbie helped her decide based on anticipated guest preferences.

Serena leaned on the island and smiled at Libbie. "I already said you're hired, right? Because if I didn't, I'm saying it now."

A tiny thrill shot through Libbie. Her first client, and one step closer to Mrs. Quincy's Labor Day party. "That's great, Serena. If it's okay with you, I'll come back in two days to finalize the menu and finish making the cocktail then."

"Sounds perfect." Serena rubbed her hands eagerly. "Something to look forward to and now I can tick 'plan promotion party' off my list." She extended an elegant hand, and Libbie noticed she wore a ring on almost every finger. "I'm so pleased you interrupted my liquid lunch. It was like a sign from the universe."

Libbie smiled uneasily at the mention of the universe, remembering Lorraine's suggestion to heed what the universe had to teach. "Yes, it was, wasn't it?"

Later that evening, after the dinner dishes had been cleared away, Libbie sat down to work on Serena Kitts' menu. She couldn't stop thinking about the recipe that had appeared while she was at the Kitts' house. She pulled out the book for another look at Serena's cocktail.

"What's that, Mom?" Courtney asked. Her daughter leaned over her shoulder for a closer look. "I like the colors. I bet I could draw something like that."

Curiosity got the better of Josh, and he came over to look. "That looks like one of the plants in your garden."

"It's rhubarb."

"Do I like rhubarb?" Courtney asked.

"I don't think you've ever had it." Libbie flipped back to her own recipe on the page before. She started to think about her herb garden and how she might improve it. That would be a good project for her while she was building her business, and it would yield fresh ingredients for her recipes—cocktails included.

She spent so long researching plants and drafting a list of those she wanted to purchase, that she failed to notice the time until the Alexa alarm sounded. "Crap, Alexa, stop." She closed her notebook and jumped out of her chair, practically colliding with Courtney. "I need to hurry and get showered before I meet the girls."

"You're going out again?" Courtney asked.

Libbie heard the note of disappointment in her daughter's voice. "I know it's my weekend, but I promise I won't be long. We need to scatter Inga's ashes."

"Can't it wait until another night when Josh and I are with Dad?"

Libbie looked into her daughter's anxious eyes and saw her younger self reflected there. "It absolutely can. Let me just text the others and let them know." There was no way Libbie could go now. Even though the kids weren't huge fans of Chris, it was still another change for them to navigate, and Libbie wanted to be supportive of her daughter's needs.

She sent a quick group text and explained the situation. They were understanding, of course, and agreed to reschedule for Wednesday night, which was Nick's next turn for an overnight. Libbie knew that Inga would understand. She'd always supported Libbie's desire to prioritize her children.

Courtney engulfed her mother in a hug. "Thanks, Mom."

"It's no problem." Libbie relished the smooth skin of her daughter's cheek pressed against hers.

"Can I go out?" Josh asked. "Hadley's having some friends over and she invited me."

"Do you need a ride?" Libbie offered.

"No, I'm good."

Courtney waited until he left the room, and a sly smile emerged. "Can we go for ice cream?"

Libbie hugged her daughter again. "Of course we can."

ELEVEN

Libbie devoted the first couple hours of her Sunday morning to grocery shopping, choosing items from her "normal" list as well as her catering list. She wanted to experiment with more recipes now that she had the time. She didn't have the money to go nuts, but she knew how to stretch a dollar thanks to years of a tight budget.

Libbie's phone vibrated, and her stomach churned when she saw the image of her mother's face on the screen. Normally she'd let it go to voicemail, but Libbie was in the mood to rip off the Band-Aid. She stopped in the produce section, next to an end cap of lemons. It seemed appropriate, given the sour taste in her mouth.

"Hi, Mom. What's up?"

"Where are you? You sound like you're in a nightclub."

*Yes, because I so often spend my Sunday morning in a nightclub.* "I'm food shopping."

"Have you found a job yet?"

"I'm not looking for a job, Mom. I'm starting my own business."

"I'm not sure that's such a good idea. You don't know the first thing about running your own business. And what about your children?"

"Good thing I didn't ask for your opinion." The words tumbled out before Libbie could stop them, although she wasn't sure that she would have anyway.

Her mother fell silent for a moment, probably unsure how to respond. It wasn't often that Libbie clapped back. She typically put up with whatever behavior her parents dumped on her, as though in agreement with the idea that Libbie somehow deserved it.

"The reason I'm calling is that we've decided to have a barbecue Thursday night. Since you're already in the store, you might as well pick up a few things so you can make the side dishes. I'm thinking a seven-bean salad would be nice. I'm tired of potato salad. And maybe vegetables for the skewers."

Nobody in the history of barbecues was ever excited to see a seven-bean salad. "I can't make it Thursday," Libbie said. "I have a catering job."

"It's just another barbecue, Elizabeth. You're hardly auditioning for Top Chef. Let them find someone else to grill their burgers."

Libbie bristled. "It isn't just another barbecue, and I don't want them to find someone else. This is a great opportunity for me." She picked up a bag of lemons and placed them in the cart. A gin and tonic suddenly seemed like a very good idea. "Is there a reason yours has to be Thursday?" It wasn't a birthday celebration; she knew that much.

"Your sister is busy the other nights this week. That was her only availability."

Naturally, they'd checked Emily's schedule first and gone ahead with the date, leaving Libbie to fit in—or not. "Well, I'm sorry. Thursday doesn't work for me."

Her mother blew out a frustrated breath. "Well, I suppose we'll have to go ahead without you. Honestly, Elizabeth, you'd think you'd want to prioritize your family now that Chris has left you."

Libbie resisted the urge to squeeze a lemon so hard that the seeds popped out. "Did it ever occur to you to plan the barbecue so *I* can come, even if Emily can't?"

Silence greeted her suggestion.

"Didn't think so."

"You're being ridiculous. I called to invite you, haven't I? It's not my fault you have plans."

"I don't have *plans*, Mom. I'm not choosing a tennis lesson over a family get-together. I have to work so that I can pay my bills."

"Maybe you should've thought of that before you quit your job or alienated another man."

Libbie closed her eyes, gathering her strength. "I need to go. It's my turn in the checkout line. I hope you all have a great time." She hung up before her mother could say another word.

Still agitated, she pushed her cart forward and broadsided another cart. "I'm so sorry!" Her eyes widened as she recognized the man behind the other cart. "Ethan. I almost didn't recognize you." Instead of a suit, he wore board shorts and a light gray T-shirt, allowing Libbie a good look at his toned arms.

Ethan broke into a wide smile at the sight of her. "This is a nice surprise." He inclined his head to the cart. "I'll have my insurance company call yours to discuss the damage."

She laughed. "I'm so sorry. I was talking to my mother."

"Ah. Say no more. How are you otherwise?"

"Good, actually. I got my first catering job." She was surprised to hear herself offer the information so freely. A few weeks ago, it was the kind of statement she would've kept to herself because it sounded too boastful.

"Congratulations. That's great news." His gaze was direct and interested. In fact, if Libbie wasn't mistaken, he seemed very interested.

Libbie felt the back of her neck grow warm. "We met with Lorraine. She was...informative. Thank you."

Ethan chuckled. "She's a character, isn't she? I probably should've warned you."

Libbie's smile melted away as she remembered what Lorraine had said about the real reason for Ethan's inquiry.

He seemed to notice her change in expression. "Is something wrong? She didn't tell you anything awful, I hope."

"No, nothing like that." She thought of the second cocktail recipe that had appeared in the book.

"Well, you look like something's on your mind." His encouraging smile remained intact, and Libbie noticed the slightest hint of a dimple in his right cheek.

Libbie glanced around to make sure no other shoppers were within earshot. "Do I need to register as a witch?"

Ethan nodded. "Actually, I should have mentioned that during our meeting. I can help you with the papers if you'd like, but I understand if you'd rather find someone else."

"Why would I want to find someone else?" she asked, a little too quickly.

"Because I'm not as well-versed as some other lawyers might be. It's not exactly something they teach in law school."

"Maybe not, but you won't get more experience without more witches as clients."

"No, I guess not." The intensity of his gaze made her whole body tingle. "Are you busy after this? Any interest in grabbing a snack at the lake instead of waiting to meet tomorrow night?"

Libbie's head jerked to attention. He sounded as eager as she felt. Then again, he probably was anxious to get the details squared away for his client party.

"I need to bring the groceries home," she said. "I can't leave them in the car in this heat."

He seemed mildly embarrassed. "No, of course not. I wasn't thinking straight."

"But I can unload my bags and meet you, if that's not too late." The prospect of sitting lakeside in his company was too tempting to pass up.

"No, that works for me. I don't need a lot. I tend to come here every few days."

"Me, too. I like to buy everything fresh."

"I guess that makes sense for a chef. How about Sandbar? I can text you when I get there."

"Sounds good to me. I'll see you then."

Libbie waited until she'd pushed her cart away to allow herself a huge smile. Even if it was only a client meeting, she had to admit she was excited to spend time alone with him. She also liked that she'd be able to talk openly with him about recent events. He was a smart guy; maybe he could offer insight into what was happening.

Even if he didn't, Libbie couldn't wait to see him again.

Sandbar had a cozier feel than a place like Pebbles, and Libbie was relieved that he'd suggested it. They sat across from each other at a small round table on the raised patio that overlooked the lake. An oversized yellow umbrella protected them from the harsh rays of the sun. The humidity was low, so they weren't bothered by the bugs that sometimes plagued the residents in the dog days of summer.

"This is perfect weather," Ethan said. "I try to spend as much time outdoors as possible when it's like this. I actually resented going food shopping."

"Why not wait until later today?"

"I have a work event."

"On a Sunday evening?" That seemed a lot to ask.

"One of my clients is celebrating his ninetieth birthday." Ethan grinned. "I tend to get invited to a lot of things. Some of my clients consider me an extension of the family, especially someone like Abe. He's a great guy. Such a fascinating life."

Libbie could understand why someone as easygoing and pleasant as Ethan was so in demand among his clients.

The server arrived and set their drinks in front of them, as well as a plate of fried crab legs to share.

"Thanks, Ashley." Libbie recognized the server from Josh's class.

"Oh, hey, Mrs. Stark." Ashley flashed a bright smile. "I didn't realize it was you. I kind of zone out when I'm waiting tables."

"Daydreaming, huh?" Libbie was familiar with that. She'd done it often enough at Basecamp, conjuring up new recipes that

Joe refused to let her try. Well, her daydreaming days were over. She was free to experiment now, and she had no intention of letting herself down.

Ashley shrugged. "Counting the hours until I can get out on the lake. I hate working and missing out on the fun."

Spoken like a true teenager. "If it's any consolation, Josh is working too."

"Yeah. I didn't mean to sound spoiled or anything."

"No worries, Ashley. Trust me, the grown-ups who are working wish they were out on the lake too. Nobody wants to toil away on a beautiful day like this."

Her head bobbed back and forth. "You're right. It is a beautiful day."

"Sunset isn't until about eight thirty. Plenty of time to enjoy it."

Ashley beamed. "Thanks, Mrs. Stark." She turned back toward the bar with a spring in her step.

"She has no idea what she's in for," Ethan said. "Endless work hours. Bills. Taxes. Insurance." He groaned. "Adulthood isn't for the weak."

"It can be overwhelming at times." Libbie bit down on a crab leg, thinking. "But then I think of Inga and remember that you can be a responsible adult and still experience genuine joy and excitement. It doesn't have to be all drudgery all the time."

Ethan clasped his hands on the table and leaned forward, lowering his voice to a conspiratorial whisper. "Tell me more about the assets Inga left you. What have you learned? I completely understand if you don't want to talk about it because it's none of my business, but I'll be honest, I'm dying to know."

"It would be a relief to have someone else to talk to about it," Libbie admitted.

"Cheers, by the way." He touched his pint glass against hers.

She smiled. "Cheers."

He tilted his head, studying her. "I have to say, whatever it is, you look radiant."

Libbie pressed the glass to her forehead in an attempt to cool the hot flash that was about to sweep over her. The heat had a way of triggering more heat—or maybe it wasn't the sun this time. Maybe it was another kind of heat all together.

"The last time anyone called me radiant, I was pregnant with Courtney." And her relentless perimenopause symptoms never let her forget that those days were basically behind her.

"Sorry, I don't know how else to put it. I mean, I thought you were beautiful when you walked into my office, but this is next level."

Libbie grew flustered. He thought she was beautiful? No one had ever referred to her as beautiful before. Not Nick or Chris, and certainly no one in her family. Emily was the beauty in their family, the one who took after their mother. Libbie was just... Libbie.

Ethan cringed as he noticed her reaction. "I'm sorry. I didn't intend to make you uncomfortable."

"No, you didn't. Honestly. It's just not an adjective I'm used to hearing." Ugh, why did she say that? She didn't want him to think she was fishing for more compliments.

His brow creased. "I probably shouldn't have said it anyway, especially if you're going to be a client. It's inappropriate."

"I'm not your client yet," Libbie said.

He perked up. "Good point. Maybe we should wait until the very end to talk about my party and any legal issues you'd like to discuss."

"That's fine with me. I can talk about the book." Libbie proceeded to tell him about the two cocktail recipes that had magically appeared and the events that had followed her consumption of the first one.

"Wow. That's quite a drink," he said.

"I know. Now I'm scrambling to make this mess I've created the best thing that ever happened to me."

"That's a great way of framing it." He nodded, smiling. "I like that a lot."

"Thanks, I can't take credit for it, though."

"Inga?"

She nodded.

"And you really think this magical cocktail you drank prompted you to make these major life changes? Not that I don't believe you, given everything I know, but it's a cocktail. It's already liquid courage."

"I don't know how to explain it." Libbie rubbed her arms, as though the movement would stimulate the right words. "I felt a spark."

"I know the feeling." Ethan's eyes glinted in the sunlight.

"Something happened when we opened the jar, and then things really took off when I drank the cocktail. I don't think it's a coincidence."

Ethan swilled his beer. "How about your friends? Have they been having the same experience?"

"No, it's strange. I seem to be the only one with pages appearing in my book. Theirs are still blank."

"Maybe it goes in alphabetical order by first name." He laughed and shook his head. "Sorry, that was a terrible attempt at a joke. To be honest, I don't know how to make sense of this."

"That makes two of us."

"Listen, there's no rush to hire me. As far as I can tell, you don't need to register right away. In fact, it might be best to wait until you have a better understanding of the magic you've inherited. Wait and see what happens with your friends."

Libbie rested her palm against her cheek. "I wish I knew more about Inga's magic so I understood mine."

"That's not how it works. It's not a direct transfer of like to like. That's why I was curious how the assets manifested."

"No, you're right. That's what Lorraine said, too." She glanced at the water where two jet skis zipped past. For the first time in years, Libbie had a strong desire to ditch the kayak and hop on a jet ski. She'd always been too afraid to ride them, although she loved the feeling of the wind in her hair and bouncing over the surface of the water.

"We should probably talk about my party," Ethan said. "I like to do a 'thank you' party every summer for my core clients. Very casual. Usually, I have it at a restaurant, but I was thinking this year I'd like to host it at my house."

"That's a lovely idea. When would you like to host it?"

"I'm flexible on the evening, as long as there's enough notice. For you and for them."

From Libbie's point of view, sooner was better than later. She had Serena's party this week, so she could certainly fit Ethan into the schedule soon afterward. "How about next Wednesday?" Nick already had the kids then, so she wouldn't need to juggle the schedule.

"I can work with that."

"How many guests, do you think?"

"Forty to fifty. I like to include the families, although most of them prefer to come without their kids. Does that sound manageable?"

"Absolutely," Libbie replied. This event would be ideal for Mrs. Quincy's requirements. Now if she could only secure one more. The clock was ticking.

"I'm open to any ideas you want to throw my way."

"I'll need to do a site visit so I can see your kitchen and the layout of your entertaining space. And the budget, of course."

"Let's set it up."

A tiny thrill shot through Libbie at the thought of spending time alone with Ethan in his home. She knew she should be more excited about the job—and she was—but she hadn't felt this way about a man in a long time. If she were being honest with herself, probably ever.

They arranged to meet at his house on Wednesday at seven. She and her friends weren't gathering until nine to scatter Inga's ashes because they'd agreed to do it under the moon and stars, just as Inga would've wanted.

Libbie was having such a good time that she was sorry to leave, but she knew she had to get moving. Hercules would need to go out and the kids would be home from work shortly. "This was nice. Thanks for inviting me."

He smiled at her in a way that made her body burst into flames. "We should probably meet again soon since we didn't really get to talk about the menu for my party."

"Yes, we definitely should."

# TWELVE

"Mom? What are you doing?"

Libbie rested on her knees in the backyard. It was Tuesday morning. After spending too much time indoors on Monday, preparing for Serena's party—including returning to the Kitts' house to finalize the menu and have Serena drink the finished cocktail—she'd decided to take advantage of another gorgeous day. Libbie was curious to see what effect the cocktail might have on Serena and was relieved when the woman decided to stick with her bartender's suggestions. Technically, Libbie could supply a bartender as labor and handle mixers and garnishes, but she couldn't provide the alcohol.

"I'm planting," she said. "Feel like digging in the dirt? I could use some help."

"Sure." Josh knelt beside her, and Libbie felt a wave of gratitude wash over her that she was blessed with a teenaged son as agreeable as Josh.

"This garden is a mess."

"Probably because you haven't been out here in ages," Josh said. "I remember when you used to spend hours out here. I'd have my Matchbox cars on the patio and would launch them into the garden when you were trying to work."

She laughed at the memory. "Probably one of the worst things you've ever done." She'd been an avid gardener at one point, but had lost interest somewhere along the way.

"What are these?" he asked, observing the trays of greenery.

Libbie waved a hand in their direction. "A variety. Some I ordered online, and some I bought locally."

"You're ordering plants online? Why not get them all at Bright Meadow?"

"Because Bright Meadow doesn't sell everything I want for this garden."

She wasn't sure how much to share with him, especially when she didn't fully understand herself. *I'm growing special herbs to make magic* would make her sound like a drug dealer. It wasn't all for the cocktail recipes, of course. She wanted certain herbs on hand for cooking.

He gestured toward a green cluster. "This one just looks like a weed. Don't you want something that looks nicer?"

"That's called *Artemisia dracunculus.* It also goes by dragon herb or tarragon. I'm planting it to protect the other plants in the garden."

"How will it do that?" Josh asked.

"It has a taste and smell that garden pests don't like, so it's a good companion plant." She wiped the beads of sweat from her brow. "That reminds me, do you know Caeden Kitts?"

"Yeah, he's a year below me at school."

"Nice kid?"

Josh shrugged. "He's okay."

Libbie looked at him. "Define 'okay.'" She sensed her son was being polite.

Josh picked up a spade and began to dig. "We don't have any friends in common."

"Who are his people? The druggies?"

Josh grunted. "Remember that kid who hid the pot in the ceiling of the boys' bathroom in a bag with his name on it?" He shook his head and laughed. "What a moron."

"That was him?" Libbie asked, aghast.

"No, but that was Caeden's best friend."

"He got suspended, though, didn't he?" Libbie tried to recall the details. She had to admit that if it wasn't her kid in trouble, she only half listened to the story.

"Yeah, so Caeden's been kind of drifting to find another crew."

Libbie nodded. It seemed like Serena Kitts' instincts were spot on. She hoped the cocktail was able to help get communication flowing between mother and son.

"You know, I'm really glad that you feel like you can talk to me."

Josh rested on his haunches, seemingly embarrassed. "You're my mom."

"I know, but you're a sixteen-year-old boy. I thought your species was supposed to be mortified by mothers."

He shrugged his lanky shoulders. "You haven't done anything to mortify me."

Libbie winked. "There's still plenty of time."

He shifted back to his knees and resumed digging. "You don't give me a hard time."

"Maybe that's because I'm too lax. Maybe I should be tougher." If she'd been tougher, maybe she'd have dumped Chris sooner and saved them all precious time.

"It's not like I do things you don't want me to do." He selected a plant from the tray and settled it into the hole. "And you always listen to me, like what I have to say is important."

Libbie's chest tightened as she realized Josh's experience was the exact opposite of her own childhood. That was probably why she made such an effort with her own kids—because of how she'd felt growing up, like she didn't matter.

"What you have to say *is* important."

Again, Libbie thought of her own experience. If your own mother doesn't think what you have to say is important, then it would be hard to convince yourself that anyone else would.

Josh smirked. "Even when I want to show you one of those memes you don't understand?"

"Even then." A short shadow passed over them, and Libbie craned her neck for a glimpse of her daughter. "Grab a spade and you can help."

Courtney glanced around the ground, and Libbie knew her fastidious child was searching for a blanket or cushion to use as a seat. Even as a toddler, she hadn't been one to play in the dirt.

"Remember when you made me that little garden to grow my own Sundrop flower?" Courtney asked.

Libbie groaned. "How can I forget?"

Josh shot her a quizzical look. "Is that the one from *Rapunzel*?"

"*Tangled*, and yes," Libbie said.

Courtney had been obsessed with the movie when she was younger, and Libbie had spent countless hours doing all sorts of Rapunzel-inspired activities. One of those activities had involved a yellow flower that Libbie had bought from the local nursery and pretended it was the Sundrop flower that had magical properties. She and Courtney had planted it together, and Libbie could still vividly recall the look of wonder in her daughter's eyes. Never mind the flower. The moment itself had been magical.

"Do you want to do anything special today since neither of you has to work?" Libbie asked.

"Can we kayak?" Courtney asked.

Her request triggered an idea. Libbie smiled. "I have a better idea. How about we rent jet skis?"

Josh perked up. "Really? But you hate them. Last time I asked, you called them aquatic death machines."

"I might have been overreacting. If you two help me plant these now, we'll have plenty of time to get on the water today."

Courtney dropped on the ground beside her mother. "Deal."

With the kids' help, Libbie was able to get the garden cleaned up and her new arrivals planted, leaving them the entire afternoon to spend on the lake. They rented two jet skis so that Josh could ride his own, and she and Courtney shared. She was glad to get

Courtney on one this young, so that she didn't develop the same fears Libbie had. It was a great day on the lake, and Libbie was grateful for this uninterrupted time with her kids. If she hadn't quit her job, she'd be working at Basecamp now and coming home tired and miserable. Instead, she was coming home exhilarated, two happy kids in tow. There was no comparison. Of course, there was still the issue of her financial future, but Libbie was feeling more optimistic with each passing day.

They arrived home and immediately let Hercules out. The kids dashed straight upstairs—to check their phones, no doubt—and Eliza came running, her tail flicking from side to side. Now that she was no longer confined to Courtney's room, Eliza seemed more comfortable in the house. A quick glance at the empty bowl indicated that the cat was hungry.

"Don't worry. I have no interest in starving you. I'm a chef. Haven't you heard? Food is kind of my specialty."

Hercules' loud bark let her know that she had company. She hoped it wasn't Chris. She was worn out from the sun and didn't have the energy to deal with him right now.

There was a knock on the screen door and Libbie heard a woman's voice. "Libbie, are you home?"

She dumped the cat food into the bowl and set the tin on the counter before making her way to the front door. "Hildie?" Libbie had known Hildie Parsons since elementary school. They'd lost touch when Libbie had gone away to college but fell back in contact after Libbie gave birth to Courtney. Hildie's son and Courtney were the same age and she and Libbie couldn't seem to show up at a Mom and Me-type event without running into one another.

"Sorry to drop by unannounced," Hildie said. "I was driving past and saw your car. Figured I'd see how you're getting on." Her sympathetic expression suggested that she knew about both Basecamp and Chris.

Libbie opened the door to let her in. "I'm doing well, thanks."

Hildie's gaze flicked over her from top to bottom. "You must mean it. You look good."

Libbie laughed. "Thanks. Can I get you a drink? It's hot out there today." She walked back to the kitchen with Hildie right behind her. Eliza bolted forward to greet their guest.

"When did you get a cat?" Hildie asked. She bent over to stroke Eliza's back.

"She was part of an inheritance," Libbie said.

Hildie straightened. "Oh, no. I'm sorry."

"Inga Paulsen. Did you know her?"

Hildie's eyes rounded. "I didn't realize you were friends with her."

Libbie nodded. "We met every week for cocktail club. Iced tea?"

"Sure." Hildie threaded her fingers on the counter. "She was an odd duck from what I'd heard. All sorts of eccentricities."

Libbie retrieved the pitcher from the fridge and two glasses. "If I'm lucky enough to live that long, I hope everyone says the same about me." She filled a glass for Hildie and passed it over to her.

"We've seen Courtney at Cone Hut and Josh at the lake. I guess they're keeping busy this summer."

"They are. What about your kids? Are they working?"

Hildie gulped down a quarter of her iced tea. Libbie didn't blame her. It was scorching outside.

"Bradley is helping out his grandfather at the hardware store, and Maya is working at the desk at the tennis club." Her gaze settled on Libbie. "How about you? Anything on the job front?"

Libbie smiled. "Actually, I've started my own business. I'm catering now." She inclined her head toward the information on the counter.

Hildie grasped the packet with eager fingers. "That's fantastic. I'm so excited for you."

"Thanks, so am I."

Hildie waved a dismissive hand. "You were too good for Basecamp anyway. That place was nothing more than a glorified diner, and Joe is as stubborn as a mule."

"I appreciate that."

Hildie flicked through the pages. "I would eat every single thing you have listed."

"That seems to be the consensus so far."

She set her hands on the counter and looked Libbie in the eye. "I can't say I'm sorry about Chris. I never said anything because it wasn't my place, but even the kids at school don't like him. Maya says he has a bad attitude, and you know it must be bad when teenagers say that." Hildie smirked. "Maya says girls are lined up trying to catch Josh's attention at the club."

"Is that so? He hasn't mentioned it." Maya was a year younger than Josh.

"He wouldn't. Too nice of a boy." Hildie winced and put a protective hand close to her armpit.

"Hildie, are you okay?"

Her grimace morphed into a smile. "Fine. Just a shooting pain. I have a bit of swelling, but I'm sure I just banged into a doorjamb or something and don't remember. Middle age will do that to a woman. I'm clumsy and forgetful all the sudden, like I had a partial lobotomy."

Libbie grew alert, remembering that Hildie's mother died from breast cancer in her forties. "Hildie," she said carefully.

"You can stop right there. I know what you're thinking."

"Do you have the gene?" Libbie asked quietly.

Hildie averted her gaze. "I don't know. I haven't been tested."

"Well, I'm sure you get annual mammograms. That's the important thing." The guilty expression on Hildie's face suggested that Libbie was wrong about that. "Wait. You don't get mammograms?"

Hildie's face grew pinched. "My schedule's busy, and you have to make the appointment with so much advanced notice. I never know what kind of time I'll have available months ahead."

"But you're having pain and swelling, Hildie. It could be an early symptom."

Hildie's eyes moistened. "I can't."

Libbie edged closer to her. "Hildie, you have a family history."

The other woman jerked toward her. "Why do you think I don't want to go? I'm terrified. I have two kids under eighteen. What if I have it?"

"Not getting diagnosed won't make it go away." Libbie placed a gentle hand on her back. "Hildie, you know bossy isn't my style."

"No, that's Kate."

Libbie allowed herself a small smile. "Exactly, but I'm telling you this. You need to go."

Hildie began to tremble. "I can't. I don't want to know."

Libbie's gaze fell on the cocktail book, now open on the counter. Odd. She didn't remember opening it. Her brow lifted when she realized there was a new entry. "I think I have something that might help you."

Hildie wiped a stray tear from her cheek. "Pot?"

"No." Libbie peered at the new recipe. "You like gin, don't you?"

"Of course. Gin is my favorite. I drink gin and tonic all summer long."

Libbie smiled. "How would you feel about a cocktail?"

Hildie shrugged. "It's five o'clock somewhere, right?"

Libbie went to the cabinet and began pulling out ingredients. "We'll sit outside, have a drink together, and talk this through."

"Thank you, Libbie. I'm so embarrassed."

"Please don't be."

"How am I going to raise two kids brave enough to face their problems when their mother is too chicken to lead by example?" Hildie shook her head. "I remember when my mom was sick. All the whispers and sad faces. It was an awful time. I remember feeling ashamed, and I didn't even know why."

Libbie listened as she mixed the ingredients of the cocktail.

The only item left was liverwort. "I'll be right back. I just need to pinch something from the garden."

"Oh, I don't need any garnish. Don't waste your plants on me."

"It's more than a garnish, and nothing can be wasted on you, Hildie Parsons." Libbie darted from the kitchen into the backyard to snip the liverwort from the garden. Liverwort, also known as hepatica, was a pretty purple flower in the buttercup family that was plentiful throughout the woods in Lake Cloverleaf. She finished mixing the cocktail and handed the finished product to her friend.

"Wow, Libbie. This looks straight out of a magazine." Hildie admired the drink, turning the glass from side to side. "You have so many talents. I can hardly keep up with them all."

"Cheers." Libbie lifted her glass of iced tea.

"Cheers." Hildie raised her glass before bringing it to her lips for a sip. She perked up as the cocktail appeared to hit her taste buds. "This is like nothing I've ever tasted."

"I hope that's a good thing."

Hildie took a longer drink this time, seeming to savor the pale purple liquid. "Oh, it's definitely a good thing." She sniffed the inside of the glass. "It even smells amazing. How do you do it?"

Libbie smiled. "Magic."

"No kidding. I wish you'd been making these back when your kids were little. I needed a stiff drink on the regular back then." She smacked her lips together. "Thank goodness we got the good eggs."

"Your kids aren't raising themselves, Hildie. They're good eggs because you're a good mom."

"Is that true though?" Hildie swallowed more of her drink. "I know good parents with bad apples. I often wonder how that happens."

"Don't discount your influence," Libbie said. "You're doing a lot of things right."

Hildie raised her glass. "Right back at you, Mom."

As if on cue, Josh and Courtney came thundering down the steps together. From the sound of it, they were debating music.

"Nirvana just sounds like someone yelling in pain," Courtney insisted. "It isn't music." She stopped short when she reached the kitchen. "Hi, Mom. Hi, Mrs. Parsons."

"Hi," Josh said.

"You two get taller every time I see you," Hildie said. "Or maybe I'm getting shorter. I swear, I'm shrinking. Another perk of middle age."

"You should try yoga," Courtney said. "It keeps your spine long. That's what the lady on YouTube tells me."

Hildie looked impressed. "You're doing yoga?"

"It was recommended," Libbie said.

"For my anxiety," Courtney added without a trace of embarrassment. She could learn a few things from her daughter, Libbie realized.

"That's a terrific idea," Hildie said. "You know what? I think I'll take a look at yoga. I'm in need of some calming methods." Her gaze flickered to Libbie, and Libbie knew she was thinking about her fleeting pain.

"What are you drinking?" Courtney asked, eyeing the cocktail. "It looks so pretty."

"Nothing for you. Not for another seven years anyway." Libbie tousled Josh's hair. "You are in definite need of a shower."

Courtney held up her hands. "I still feel sticky from the lake. It doesn't matter how many times I wash my hands."

"Why don't you two get showers?" Libbie suggested. "You're old enough to do that without being told."

"What's in it for me?" Courtney asked.

Hildie laughed. "A shrewd negotiator. I like it."

"You like to be clean and you hate seaweed in your hair. That's what's in it for you," Libbie said.

They took off for the staircase, and Hercules bounded after them.

"I hope you don't mind me saying this, but your house feels lighter," Hildie said, once they were out of earshot.

She knew Hildie meant the absence of Chris. "I think so, too," she agreed.

"And everything's good with Nick?"

"As good as things can possibly be with your ex."

Hildie finished the remainder of her cocktail and even sucked down the ice cubes. "Thanks for this, Libbie. It was a feast for the senses."

"Wow, I'm putting that on my marketing material."

Hildie laughed. "I wish I needed a caterer. You'd be top of the list."

"If you hear of anyone, will you pass along my information? I could use the recommendations."

"Absolutely." Hildie placed her empty glass in the sink. "Thank you for your hospitality. Hope to see you again before summer's over."

Libbie escorted her friend to the door. "Let me know what happens, okay?"

Hildie answered with a vague smile, and Libbie hoped that meant she would at least call for an appointment. One funeral this summer was quite enough.

"I'll be in touch," Hildie said.

Libbie leaned against the doorframe with a heavy heart and watched her friend drive away. She knew the situation could easily be reversed. No one in the world was guaranteed good health or even happiness for that matter.

*You have to appreciate what you have when you have it*, Libbie thought and quickly realized it was something she'd heard Inga say. It hadn't really registered until now. It seemed to Libbie that her old friend had planted and watered a lot of seeds these past few years. It saddened Libbie to know she was no longer here to watch them grow.

Libbie returned to the kitchen and took a closer look at the recipe that had appeared for Hildie. She was lucky to have had the herb she needed in her garden. It occurred to her that she needed to do more than simply plant new herbs in the garden. She needed to understand them as a...well, as a witch. She searched on her phone for 'magical herbs.' She wasn't sure what she expected to find, but she was pleasantly surprised to discover a variety of books on the subject. She ordered two of them with her Prime subscription. Inga's book was assisting her in mysterious ways, but there was no reason why Libbie couldn't do homework on her own to better understand the ingredients. There was no guarantee the book would produce a recipe for everyone. What if Libbie decided she needed a cocktail to help a friend and the book didn't come through? She wanted to make sure she had the knowledge and supplies for an assortment of possibilities.

Libbie sat at the table with her iced tea, and Eliza jumped up on the chair next to her. "You know what?" she said to the cat. "I don't even know how the cocktail was meant to help Hildie."

It wasn't as though the recipe would cure cancer. If it was capable of that, then there'd be no need for radiation and mastectomies. She searched online for the herb she'd used in Hildie's cocktail, and the intended effect quickly became clear.

Hepatica is well-known in magical circles to inspire confidence and trust.

Libbie nodded thoughtfully. That seemed exactly what Hildie needed—to have enough confidence and trust to overcome her fear.

She bonked Eliza on the nose, and the cat meowed in response. "We're going to educate ourselves, Eliza. If I'm to be a witch, then I intend to be the best witch I can possibly be."

# THIRTEEN

By the time Wednesday rolled around, Libbie felt a little of her old anxiety sliding back into focus. She was going to be alone with Ethan at his house this evening. At least there was another demand on her time, so she wasn't in danger of overstaying her welcome. She was meeting her friends at nine to scatter Inga's ashes, and there was no way she'd ask them to reschedule a second time.

She spent most of the day prepping for the Kitts' party and making sure she ticked every item off her list that she possibly could.

Somewhere in the house, Hercules barked. Libbie heard the sound of the front door open, and her breathing hitched when Chris swaggered into the kitchen.

"What are you doing here?" she asked.

"Picking up my stuff."

"You should've called first."

He shrugged. "Thought you might hang up on me or say no."

"You're lucky I didn't leave everything outside to rot."

His brow lifted. "That's a little aggressive for you, Lib." He noticed a bottle of brandy on the counter and came over to investigate. "Day drinking? That's not really your style. I guess you're taking this breakup harder than you've been pretending."

"It's for a recipe," she said.

"You're a bartender now? I thought you were a caterer."

Libbie's gaze darted to Inga's book that was open on the counter.

"What's this?" He reached for the book, and Libbie snatched it away.

"None of your business."

He laughed. "Is this the nice suburban lady's version of a meth lab?"

"Don't be ridiculous." She clutched the book to her chest. "Can you please get your things and go? I have a lot to do."

Chris grunted. "Yeah, I heard all about your fancy catering business. It was stupid of you to quit your job."

Libbie looked him dead in the face. "It seems I've done a number of stupid things in the past three years."

Chris laughed. "Well, you can add catering business to the list. How long do you think this will last? I bet you don't make it through the summer before you're begging one of the restaurants to hire you."

Libbie felt her blood begin to simmer. "What's that supposed to mean?"

"Do you really think you can run a business by yourself? It was one thing to have Joe as your boss. You're not really the type to put yourself out there."

"Do you seriously think I'm less capable than he is?"

Chris shrugged. "I guess time will tell. Where's my stuff?"

"In the boxes in the hallway upstairs."

"Sweet of you to pack for me."

"The faster you leave."

He strode past her and went upstairs, returning a minute later with the first two boxes. "You should be hurling dishes at me right now. Why are you so calm?" His face lit up. "Oh, I get it. I bet you've got a bottle of Xanax hidden somewhere in here, don't you?"

"I don't need Xanax, Chris. I only needed clarity."

"And you got that, did you?"

Libbie met his gaze with confidence. "Yes."

His brow creased. "Aren't you even going to ask me why?"

She shifted her attention back to the recipe, wishing he would just get his boxes and go. "It doesn't matter why."

"I thought women were big on closure."

"I don't need to rely on someone else to give me what I need."

He observed her for a long moment, as though he wanted to say more. It probably rattled him that she didn't lose her temper or cry or demand answers. The truth was that she didn't care what his reasons were. His behavior was about him, not about her. She could only control how she reacted to the situation.

"Suit yourself. I'll be back in a sec for the rest." He carried two boxes through the house to the car outside and returned a few minutes later for two more. He seemed to be deliberately dragging it out. Libbie knew what was in those boxes and none of them were particularly heavy, certainly not for someone as muscular as Chris.

He threw open the door when he returned for more boxes and it slammed into the wall. She knew he was trying to get a rise out of her, but she refused to take the bait. She simply stood there and watched him with a blank expression.

"I heard you went to see a lawyer," Chris said. "I guess he told you there's no case against me."

"The lawyer has nothing to do with you." Libbie focused on her ingredients. Serena's party was far more important than scoring points in a fight.

"I should've known. You never fight back. It's so boring. I should've left you a long time ago." When she failed to respond, he made a scoffing sound. "Whatever. Have fun being liberated." He made air quotes for 'liberated.'

Libbie ignored him, unwilling to engage in an argument. It wasn't worth the energy. *He* wasn't worth the energy. Thank God she didn't have children with him. He would've made a terrible father, and she would've grown to resent him that much faster. At least Nick was a good dad and a decent ex-husband. Their relationship wasn't perfect—never was—but it wasn't a train wreck. Nick's marriage to Olivia helped. Libbie suspected his wife played a major role in their continued civility.

"Have a nice life, Elizabeth." He struggled to open the door this time, and Libbie rushed over to help. The sooner he was gone, the better.

"I got it." His tone was testy. He resented her opening a door for him, but he'd been perfectly happy to let her do all the heavy lifting during their three years together. Ironic.

"Good luck to you," she said. Three years of her life and 'good luck to you' was all she wanted to say as he left. He might as well have been a complete stranger.

He gave her one last resentful look before leaving the house. She didn't watch him go. Instead, she returned to the kitchen to focus on what she could control. The menu.

She heard the squeal of tires as he pulled out of the driveway faster than necessary. He had the maturity of a high school boy. It wouldn't surprise her to learn that he'd keyed her car. He'd broken her trust and stolen thousands of dollars from her, yet he somehow acted as though he stood on higher ground.

"What was I thinking?" she murmured.

The truth was she hadn't been thinking. She'd been a passenger in her life, watching the world whiz past as she went through the motions of what she was supposed to do. Well, there would be no more 'supposed to.' Libbie was ready to start living life on her own terms, no matter how much it terrified her.

She spent an inordinate amount of time in front of the mirror that evening in preparation for her meeting with Ethan. In a desperate moment, she called Kate for advice on her outfit.

"You need to come straight to the woods afterward, so you have to find something that works in both venues." Kate laughed. "Good luck with that."

In the end, she settled on neatly pressed, light gray shorts and a black short-sleeved blouse that matched the color of her hair. She did what she could with makeup but was surprised to see that her skin didn't seem as blotchy as she remembered. She even put on a silver bracelet for good measure, something she wouldn't have bothered to do for a night out with Chris.

She sang the whole way over to Ethan's house. The radio station was playing 80s music, and Libbie was afraid she'd lose her voice by the time she arrived.

Libbie took a moment to admire the home's exterior before walking up to the front door. It had a more contemporary feel than the traditional lake houses with its dark gray siding mixed with stone.

Ethan answered the door, freshly showered and out of his suit, and Libbie's heart dipped at the sight of his slightly damp hair. There was a wave to it now that she hadn't seen before.

"Right on time." He gestured for her to enter.

Libbie tried not to walk through the house with her mouth open. The house was much nicer than she'd envisioned. She'd pictured a bachelor pad with mismatched furniture and clashing decor, but this was clearly a home with style.

She paused in front of a room-divider wine rack attached to the industrial-style bar. "This is great."

He beamed as though he'd made it with his own two hands. "Isn't it? One of my favorite features of the house, aside from the fireplace and the view, of course." He motioned to the wine bottle on the bar. "Care for a drink?"

"That would be great." Libbie thought one drink would be a good idea. As much as she enjoyed her newfound confidence, she worried that it would dissipate in Ethan's presence.

"I like what you've done with your hair," he said, as he poured the wine.

"I brushed it." Inwardly, she cringed. Was that the best she could do? "Sorry, that sounded flippant. I get anxious around people I don't know well." *And sometimes around people I do*, she thought.

"Funny." He handed her a glass of red wine. "You strike me as a confident woman."

"I'm an anxious person, always have been. When I was eleven, I started worrying about trash. My mother told me it would pass, but it didn't. I still worry about everything, from the rainforest to the polar ice caps to people in nursing homes without visitors." She shrugged and sipped her wine. "Although I've been much better recently, and I credit the cocktail recipe in Inga's book."

"I don't doubt you."

He offered her a tour of the space available for the party, and Libbie designed the layout of the tables and serving areas in her head. The deck was wonderful. It had the same modern aesthetic as the rest of the house but with the same beautiful, albeit traditional, view. They discussed the menu, and he rubber-stamped everything she proposed. Libbie felt incredibly lucky to have met him when she did.

"Now that we're done talking business..." she began. They stood on the deck enjoying the setting sun.

His mouth twitched in amusement. "Are we? I wasn't sure."

She cast him a sidelong glance. "Do you mind if I ask you a personal question?"

"Sure." His expression was so open and honest, his gaze direct without inching into creep territory.

Libbie hadn't drawn a comparison before, but it occurred to her that Chris tended to avoid eye contact with her, probably because he'd had something to hide. Libbie froze as a realization swept over her. No, that wasn't right. Chris didn't avoid eye contact with her. *She* had avoided eye contact with *him*. In fact, she realized she didn't feel comfortable looking anyone in the eye. Direct eye contact had always been a source of anxiety for her. Yet, here she was, gazing straight at Ethan Townsend's face and enjoying every second of it. Was this the magical cocktail at work or Ethan's own brand of magic—or both?

"I hope this isn't too intrusive, but what happened to your sister? Deb, right?"

Ethan glanced away, and Libbie was worried that she'd ruined their moment. "Car accident," he said. "They thought she was going to make it." He paused to sip his wine. "She lasted two weeks, but the damage was too extensive."

"I'm sorry." Instinctively she reached for him and placed a comforting hand on his arm. "You weren't able to talk to her?"

"No, she had a breathing tube and..." He stopped, frowning. "How did you know?"

Heat flooded her cheeks. "Lorraine might've mentioned that you had questions for your sister. I'm sorry. I didn't mean to be intrusive."

To her great relief, he smiled. "It's okay. I should've told you that was the reason I sought her out. I guess I was embarrassed. Lawyers are supposed to seek answers from the facts and the law, not the spiritual realm."

"You're dealing with witches now, Ethan. I don't think you should worry about what a typical lawyer would do."

"Yeah, you're right. Deb was my older sister. She was the one I went to for advice. There was a lot I didn't know."

"What about your parents?"

"That was one of the questions I had for her." He swallowed hard. "We were adopted, you see, and Deb had done the research on our biological parents a few years ago."

Libbie's hands returned to her glass. "Oh, wow. And she found them?"

He nodded. "But I didn't want to know. At the time, I felt like it was a slap in the face of our adoptive parents. They're terrific parents and I guess I felt..."

"Guilty?" Libbie offered.

"Yeah. I also worried about our biological parents. What if we discovered they'd had more kids that they kept? Or what if I my mother didn't want to meet me? I don't know. There was so much about it that scared me, so I let Deb do her thing and told her not to tell me."

"And, like a good sister, she honored your request."

"Too well. I searched everywhere after she died, and I couldn't find any trace of her research. I found her Lisa Frank sticker book, for Pete's sake, but no sign of the adoption information."

"Ooh. Did she have the liquid stickers? Those were my favorites."

"Unicorns, music notes. You name it, it's in the book."

Libbie still had her book in a box somewhere. She'd have to hunt for it. It was the kind of thing Courtney might like to see. "And was Lorraine able to contact your sister?"

His lips pressed together. "She was."

Libbie brightened. "Amazing. So you were able to say every-thing you wanted to say?" That had to be a relief given the tragic circumstances.

"I asked for the basics about them. I know they're not together because they live in different states, but that's about it."

"Wait, you still haven't contacted them?"

His gaze flicked toward the lake. "I haven't worked up the nerve."

"Then why reach out to Lorraine?"

He shrugged. "Baby steps. With Deb gone, it sort of kicked me in the ass to want the information. I just haven't found the courage to do anything with it yet."

Her heart ached for him. It had to be excruciating. Knowing he had family out there but being too afraid to reach out to them. As someone with her own kind of rejection and abandonment issues, she understood the dilemma.

"Courage seems to be in ample supply these days, so maybe yours will come." Her eyes widened. "Hold on." She returned to the kitchen where she'd left her belongings. In her tote bag was Inga's book.

"You have a curious glint in your eye, Libbie Stark." Ethan had followed her into the house.

She flipped open the book but there was no new cocktail recipe on the page. She wondered whether the recipe that had given her so much courage would do the same for him. It was worth a try.

"How about another drink? I think I have enough time to make one."

Ethan set his empty wine glass on the island. "I don't have anywhere to be, and the company's pretty good."

Libbie went through the list of ingredients to make sure he had everything she needed. In a normal cocktail, she'd be happy to substitute, but she assumed this kind needed to be precise. He watched as she worked, asking a question here or there. To her surprise, she didn't find it annoying to have Ethan hovering. She'd hated when Nick and Chris stood behind her in the kitchen. She'd felt like she was under scrutiny. With Ethan, it felt different. She felt like she was being admired.

When she finally finished, Libbie handed him the cocktail, and he gave it a curious look. "And what will this do? Will I fall asleep until a princess comes to offer true love's kiss?"

"That's a fairy tale. Honestly, I don't know if it will do anything at all. I'm still figuring this out."

"Promise me I won't develop a fin that forces me to live in the lake."

"It might do nothing except taste good. Just because I'm now a witch doesn't mean everything I make is magic."

"I don't know. I've seen your recipes. I beg to differ."

He sniffed the liquid. "If you give me the recipe, can I make it for myself?"

"You can, but I get the sense if anything magical is going to happen, then I have to make it. I don't think it's a simple matter of mixing the ingredients." A hint of a smile touched her lips. "It's more witchology than mixology."

He took a hesitant sip and smacked his lips together. "Hey, it's really tasty."

"Drink all of it. That's the best way to make sure it's effective."

He raised an eyebrow. "Trying to get me drunk, Ms. Stark?"

"If one of these gets you drunk, I'd say we need to work on your tolerance level."

He laughed and swallowed more of the cocktail. "I appreciate you taking the time to do this." He polished off the rest of the golden liquid and set the empty glass on the counter. "I have to admit, I feel a little buzzed. It's probably best if I don't operate any heavy machinery."

"I'm really sorry," Libbie said, "but I need to go now."

"I'm sorry, too. It's been fun."

Libbie was pleased to hear a note of disappointment in his voice.

He walked her to the door, and Libbie's chest throbbed at the thought of him kissing her good night. He wouldn't, of course. This wasn't a date. It was only a professional meeting. Still, the fantasy of his lips on hers was too good to ignore.

"Thank you, Libbie. I'm really looking forward to seeing you again." The look in his eye was unmistakable. Desire.

"Same." Very much the same.

As she turned and walked to her car, Libbie could've sworn her feet struck the ground with each step, but anyone who was watching would've told her that she was floating on air. It was as though love itself was a fifth element, a force powerful enough to counteract gravity.

# FOURTEEN

Libbie smiled and hummed to herself, the windows down as she drove to Parsons Ridge, where she'd arranged to meet the other women. She saw three silhouettes in the moonlight as she parked.

"Where were you?" Julie asked, as Libbie exited her car. "I drove by your house to see if you wanted a lift, but your car wasn't there."

"I was with a client." She'd opted not to tell the other two women about Ethan, or they'd never make it to the woods. Julie and Rebecca would want to conduct a full investigation of the matter.

Kate made a noise at the back of her throat but said nothing.

"Are we ready?" Libbie asked.

Kate held up the jar and shook the contents. "Say hello to my little friend."

Libbie went over and kissed the jar. "Hello, you beautiful witch."

"Someone's in a good mood," Rebecca said.

"I have two catering jobs booked. One to go, and I'll be showing up on Mrs. Quincy's doorstep to finalize the menu."

"That's so great," Julie said. "We're really proud of you."

"All of us," Kate said, tilting her head toward the jar.

"I didn't find anything specific we need to say or do," Kate said, as they walked toward the overlook. It had been one of Inga's favorite hiking spots, and the women knew she'd be at peace here.

Libbie stared at the scenic landscape and sighed with contentment. "Thank you, Inga. I love you."

They each took a turn with the jar, spreading the ashes around them.

"Should we head back to my house for drinks?" Rebecca asked.

"I think Inga would insist on it," Kate agreed.

Twenty minutes later, the women gathered around the wrought-iron table on Rebecca's patio with a round of drinks. Libbie kept wiping the condensation from her glass onto her shorts. It was her favorite kind of summer evening—warm with low humidity, no bugs trying to drain the alcohol from her blood, and good friends to laugh with. Summer nights were so peaceful here, despite the influx of tourists.

"Do you think we count as a coven because there are four of us?" Julie asked.

"I don't want to be a coven," Kate said. "It conjures up images of hunch-backed crones and bony fingers."

Rebecca polished off her cocktail and bit down on a piece of ice. "I think we should just be the cocktail club, same as we were."

"But we're not the same as we were," Libbie said quietly. Her gaze was fixed on the string of colorful lights strung through the trees that gave the outdoor space a warm, inviting glow.

"Speak for yourself," Julie said. "We haven't all been graced with Inga's gifts."

"Seriously," Rebecca chimed in. "The only change I'm grappling with is the same one we all are. Starts with 'm' and ends with 'enopause.'"

"Technically, it starts with 'p,'" Kate said.

"Do you know my phone doesn't even recognize the word?" Rebecca asked, outraged. "It always autocorrects to 'Perry menopause.' I mean, who in the hell is Perry Menopause?"

Julie pressed her cup to her forehead. "Just saying the word triggered a hot flash."

"I think summer is triggering your hot flash: The hotter it gets outside, the hotter my body gets inside. If I die a middle-aged woman, I'd better not go to Hell or it's going to be..." Kate trailed off.

"Hell?" Libbie offered.

Rebecca rolled her eyes. "Oh, please. I wish I was having hot flashes. They're the lesser of two evils."

Libbie cast her a sidelong look. "What's worse than hot flashes?"

Rebecca raised an open palm. "Hi. My name is Rebecca, and I'm on day eleven-thousand-and-thirty. My period doesn't know if it's coming or going."

Julie released a weighty breath. "I don't know. I'm so tired of being a different temperature from everyone else in the room. Whoever said men are from Mars and women are from Venus wasn't talking about middle-aged women. We're definitely the Red Planet, or better yet Mercury, because that's closer to the sun."

Kate tossed a handful of nuts at each of them. "You get a menopause badge, and you get a menopause badge."

Libbie laughed as she managed to catch a couple of nuts. It was so nice to have friends who understood and commiserated with what she was going through. If she had to deal with these changes alone—all the recent changes, not just menopause—she wasn't sure she could do it.

Rebecca groaned. "My mood swings more than wealthy New Yorkers in the seventies."

Julie waved her hands emphatically. "Okay, okay. Before we get too drunk. Compliment circle."

"Now?" Rebecca asked.

"We haven't done one since the night that Inga..." Julie trailed off.

Kate smacked the table with both hands. "Julie's right. We're overdue."

Rebecca wiggled her empty cup. "Can I wait until I refill?"

"No, let's do it first, then you can fill up the tank," Julie said.

They set down their cups and joined hands.

"I'll go first," Libbie said.

Kate's eyes widened. "Wow, you really have changed."

Libbie glared at her best friend. "Don't make me feel self-conscious about it." She straightened in her chair. "Lay it on me, ladies."

"I'll start," Kate said. "You inspire me, Libbie. You've been so courageous since Inga died. I'll be honest, I never thought you'd be willing to make changes to your life. You're surprising the hell out of me, and I'm here for it."

"You're bringing a whole new meaning to 'change of life,'" Rebecca agreed.

"You gave your mother pushback," Kate said. "That's huge." She looked at their other two friends. "This is the woman who routinely puts everyone else's needs ahead of her own."

Julie smirked behind her glass. "We've met her, you know."

But Kate was on a roll. "Remember that time you had an appendectomy and were so uncomfortable in bed, but you wouldn't move Hercules from his spot because you felt bad? You were in such pain, but you still prioritized the dog's needs over your own."

"I'd probably still do that," Libbie admitted.

"Me, too," Rebecca said. "You'd understand if you liked dogs, Kate."

Kate swept her hair back off her shoulder. "Okay, missing the point."

"My turn," Julie said, wiggling in her seat. "You are one awesome lady. You're showing your kids how to live their best lives, and that's an even greater gift than the one Inga left you."

"Left *us*," Libbie reminded her.

"I'll believe it when I see it," Julie shot back. "My book is still blank, my friend."

Rebecca cleared her throat, signaling her turn. "You're a great friend. With everything you have going on right now, you still make time for us."

Libbie beamed. "Thank you all. I appreciate your kind words."

Kate gaped at her. "Look at that. You're not even blushing."

Libbie touched her cheeks. "They feel warm."

"That's the alcohol," Julie said.

"Or a hot flash," Rebecca added.

They continued around the circle, each woman getting her turn as the recipient of compliments. By the end, Libbie felt more uplifted than she had in ages.

"I'm so glad Inga forced us to partake in that little ritual," Kate said. "Now it's ingrained as a habit."

"I started doing it with my kids without thinking about it," Libbie said. "It sort of spilled over into my other interactions."

Kate nodded. "She was such an inspiration. I wish I could've persuaded her to appear on my channel. It would be nice to have preserved her online."

"She wasn't interested in the spotlight," Libbie said. *Like me.*

"I'll make the next round," Kate said. She scooted back her chair and walked over to the butler's tray that doubled as a bar.

Libbie watched as her friend held up the jigger to the light to make sure her measurement was accurate.

"Just dump it in," Rebecca called. "No one cares."

"I care," Kate sniffed.

Kate's perfectionist tendencies had started young. Her parents divorced when she was eight, and her mother later committed suicide when Kate was fifteen. Her mother asked her to go to the store for milk and, by the time Kate returned with the purchase, her mother was gone.

Libbie leaned over to Rebecca and whispered, "Just let her do it."

"The lady from *Titanic* was faster throwing her necklace in the ocean," Julie complained.

Kate glared at her as she returned with the first two drinks and then went back for the other two. "No one's dying of thirst here."

"No, but I might die from lack of alcohol," Julie shot back.

"I can't drink too much because of Serena's party tomorrow," Libbie said.

"Good luck with that," Rebecca said. "We're rooting for you."

"Thanks." They toasted to Inga, and Libbie finished half her cocktail before declaring the night over. She was relieved that the other women didn't give her a hard time. She would've liked to stay, but duty called.

She left the house feeling buoyant and tilted back her head to admire the night sky. She couldn't remember the names of the constellations. She'd have to ask Josh tomorrow. He'd always been interested in astronomy from the time he'd started to read.

She slipped behind the wheel and drove home.


Libbie stood at the island in the kitchen, feeling completely in control. It was an amazing sensation, and she relished every second of it. On the drive over, she was convinced she'd suffer from a nervous stomach or have a strong desire to hide in the pantry, but, once she got settled in the Kitts' kitchen, she realized that the opposite had occurred. She was in her element.

"Everything looks and smells amazing," Serena said. She looked beautiful with her hair pulled back in a twist. Gold earrings studded with diamonds dangled from her lobes.

"Thank you," Libbie said. "You look stunning."

Serena brightened. "Aren't you sweet?" She glanced around, as though afraid of being overheard, though the guests weren't due to arrive for another forty-five minutes. "I have to know. What was in that cocktail you made me? It was a life-altering experience."

Libbie met Serena's earnest gaze. "You saw the recipe. Just a few basic ingredients."

"I have to tell you." Serena's voice dropped to a whisper. "I felt so empowered after I drank the cocktail that when Caeden came home, I sat him down, and we had the best talk we've ever had."

Libbie's spirits lifted. "That's great news. I'm so happy for you."

"It started out in the usual way. You know, me asking a basic question and him grunting a reply, but then something amazing happened. It was like my brain knew the right thing to say to encourage him to open up and, before I knew it, we were having a genuine conversation. Actual words strung together that formed coherent statements."

Libbie didn't have to pretend to be amazed. "That's fantastic."

Serena wagged a playful finger at her. "I think that cocktail of yours gave me the liquid courage I needed."

As far as Libbie was concerned, it seemed to offer a lot more than that. "And what did you find out? Nothing horrible, I take it?"

"Not at all. In fact, he was telling me about the work he's been doing. All this time I thought he was doing drugs and watching porn, but he's actually been drawing illustrations using an app on his phone and, let me tell you, they are amazing." She clasped her hands and emitted a dreamy sigh. "He wants to apply to art schools. Of course, his father will throw a tantrum at the prospect of paying for an education in the arts, but I wholly support it."

Libbie was thrilled for the Kitts. She hoped that Serena continued to keep the lines of communication open with her son.

"My daughter uses a similar app," Libbie said. "She's drawn some incredible pictures with it."

Serena broke into a wide smile. "Really? So you have a budding artist, too? That's wonderful."

"She's very talented."

"Is she in any special classes? I was thinking I might do a little research and see whether Caeden is interested. It would be nice to get him to be a part of something. He seems to spend so much time alone." She laughed lightly. "As you've probably guessed, I'm more of an extrovert."

"Courtney doesn't like the formal structure of an art class. She said she prefers to follow her own muse."

Serena slapped a hand against her chest in dramatic fashion.

"Oh, to be young and have a muse. I'm so jealous. My only muse these days is the *Vogue* beauty editor. I don't know her at all, but she really seems to get me."

The timer beeped, and Libbie turned to remove the trays of crab puffs from the oven. Her special ingredient was a dash of cayenne pepper. When she'd made the puffs for Chris's birthday last year, he'd seen the ingredients on the counter and asked why she didn't just throw hot sauce in there, as well. Of course, he didn't complain once he tasted them. No one could. They were small heavenly clouds in your mouth.

"And here's my young Matisse now." Serena smiled as a surly young man entered the kitchen. His shaggy brown hair seemed at odds with his shirt and tie and neatly pressed trousers. "Caeden, this is Libbie Stark, Josh's mother. He's a year ahead of you at school."

Caeden gave an awkward nod. "Yeah, I know who he is."

"I was telling Libbie about your artwork. Why don't you show her some of your drawings?"

"Mom, I asked you not to tell anyone." Caeden's face was a reddened mixture of embarrassment and pride.

"Oh, stop. My son's talents aren't meant to be hidden away. They're to be celebrated."

He rolled his eyes. "Please don't tell everyone at the party. I don't want to spend half the day holding up my phone."

"Why not? You do that anyway." Serena winked at him.

Caeden scrolled on his screen and turned it so Libbie could see a picture of a dragon with sparkling green scales and a soulful expression.

"Wow. That's amazing, Caeden. I bet you've got dozens of layers there."

He perked up at the mention of layers. "I do. Probably about fifty."

"How long did it take you to draw that?"

"About five days. I mean, I'm not drawing all day every day, but I definitely spent hours each day."

"That takes a lot of patience and commitment," Libbie said.

"That's what I told my husband," Serena said. "Caeden has plenty of discipline when it's something he actually wants to do."

Another timer dinged, and Serena patted her son's shoulder. "We should get out of Libbie's hair now. I'm sure she has plenty left to do before the guests arrive."

"Thank you for sharing your picture with me," Libbie said. "You should be very proud of it."

Caeden offered a shy smile. "Thanks."

"The next time you're at the club, you should say hi to Josh. He's working there as a lifeguard most days." Most of the teenagers in town spent at least a couple days a week at the club, those without jobs anyway.

"I will." Caeden turned and left the kitchen, still wearing the same smile.

The moment they left, Libbie switched into business mode. Her energy level was high, and she was relieved to notice she felt positive rather than anxious. Even when the doorbell rang announcing the first guest, Libbie didn't flinch. She simply carried on with the preparations, humming to herself as she worked.

Pretty soon the house was teeming with guests, and Libbie only paused to rest once the party was in full swing. She sank into the shadows to observe the merriment. Everything seemed to be going well. The food and drinks were flowing, and people were chatting and eating happily. The back doors were wide open so the outdoor patio felt like it was integrated with the rest of the house.

Libbie didn't want to get her hopes up, but she knew if she could impress the guests, maybe that would lead to another job. She still needed a third under her belt, sooner rather than later, to satisfy Mrs. Quincy and, ultimately, the mortgage company.

A familiar figure cut through the cluster of guests in front of the doorway, and Libbie drew a sharp intake of breath. Ethan's hair was slightly ruffled from the breeze, and she realized he must've been one of the guests on the patio. He smiled when he spotted her and strode to greet her.

"I didn't know you'd be here." Libbie suddenly wished she'd taken more pains with her appearance. She probably had flour smudges on her face.

"You mentioned a catering job, but it didn't occur to me it might be this one." He shook his head. "I should've asked. Compliments to the chef, by the way. The food has been nothing short of amazing."

The old Libbie would've minimized her involvement, as though the ingredients had miraculously organized and cooked themselves. The new Libbie, however, simply said, "Thank you."

"I only realized it was you because someone outside asked about the chef, and I heard your name." He glanced over his shoulder to the patio. "Honestly, I never would've stepped foot inside otherwise. It's gorgeous out there today."

"I'm glad. Good weather puts everyone in the right frame of mind for a party."

"I wish you could join us. It would make a good party even better."

Libbie didn't have a chance to respond. Serena swept past them and plucked a clean martini glass from the counter. "Have you two met?"

"Actually, we have," Ethan said. "Through work."

Serena placed a manicured hand on his shoulder. "Ethan is a marvelous attorney. If you're in the market, I highly recommend him. More importantly, my husband recommends his services, and he's a real pain in the ass to please. Aren't you, darling?"

Matthew Kitts moved into Libbie's view and wrapped both arms around his wife's waist. "Are you disparaging me in front of the guests?"

She tapped his forehead with the base of her glass. "It's more entertaining than doing it privately."

"It's true," he said, looking at Libbie. "I am a pain in the ass. Very hard to please. Thankfully I have a wife who puts up with me." He gave her a firm kiss on the cheek.

Serena patted her husband's cheek and smiled. "We deserve each other. We have to. No one else would tolerate us."

Libbie softened as she watched their interaction. As much as Serena complained about him, she seemed to genuinely love her husband.

"Congratulations on your promotion," Libbie said.

"Thank you. I put in a lot of hours, so it's nice to be rewarded." Matt snaked his arm around his wife and clasped her hand. "I believe you owe me a dance, fair lady."

They sauntered out of the kitchen, arm-in-arm.

"I guess you're too busy for dancing on the patio," Ethan said.

"Afraid so."

"I have an idea. Why don't you come over for dinner one night? I'll cook, so you don't have to. We'll do it after my party, so there's no professional conflict."

"What about the witch registration?"

He waved a hand. "I refuse to represent you, but I'm more than happy to find you someone who can."

Libbie's spirits soared. A kind, handsome man wanted to cook dinner for her. Ethan Townsend was exactly the type of man she didn't know she wanted until now. "I'd love to...but I can't."

"Oh, okay." Ethan seemed to take it in stride.

"It isn't that I don't want to. I do." She really, really did. "But I jumped into a marriage, and then I jumped into my last relationship without really thinking about whether it was the right relationship for me. Without working on myself first. I don't want to repeat the pattern."

"Well, from where I'm seated, you don't need much work, but I know that's a personal decision." He smiled. "If you change your mind, you know where to find me."

Libbie's gaze lingered on him for another long moment. She didn't realize she could feel this attracted to a man at her age. She hadn't felt this drawn to someone, even when she was in her prime.

Wait. What if she were in her prime *now*?

"Libbie?"

She snapped to attention. "Sorry."

"Are you running through all the reasons why you should change your mind?" He flashed a hopeful grin.

She reached over and squeezed his arm. "You'll be the first to know. I promise. You should go mingle before they miss you."

Ethan reluctantly left the kitchen, and Libbie tried to focus on the job. Part of her couldn't believe she'd just turned him down. She'd waited her whole life to meet someone like Ethan and, even better, he seemed as interested in her as she was in him.

She didn't have long to dwell on it because Serena hurried toward her, followed by an older woman in a deep purple kaftan. Her silver hair was styled in a French twist, and emerald studs adorned her earlobes.

"Here she is," Serena said with a bright smile. "Libbie Stark, I'd like you to meet Mrs. Frankie Smith. She's been raving about the food, so I thought an introduction was in order."

Frankie shook her hand. "I don't know what you put in your puffs, but it tastes like a miracle in my mouth."

Serena nudged her. "I bet you've never said that to your husband."

Frankie laughed. "Oh, Serena. Such wicked thoughts in that beautiful head of yours." She shifted her attention to Libbie. "I understand this is a new business venture for you."

"That's right."

"It just so happens I have an event coming up, and my usual caterer broke his leg in a water-skiing accident. I've been asking around, but all the good ones are booked this far into summer." Her lips curved into a smile. "Well, all the good ones save one, I hope."

"When's the event?" Libbie asked.

"Two weeks," Frankie said. "Why don't you come by the house this week, and we can discuss the menu? I can tell you right now that those puffs are definitely going to be on it."

Libbie felt a sense of pride. She'd devised that recipe on her own after many subpar experiments, so its success was satisfying.

"I'm happy to share her now that our event is almost over," Serena said.

"I understand you worked at Basecamp before this." Frankie scrunched her nose. "I never would've had the pleasure of tasting your food there. The menu didn't appeal to me."

"Their loss is Lake Cloverleaf's gain," Serena said. "Be warned. She also makes a cocktail that will change your life."

Frankie shot Libbie a curious look. "Is that so? Well, I am always in the market for a mind-blowing cocktail."

"They're customized for the individual," Libbie said. "We can talk about it more when we meet to discuss your event."

"Sounds good to me."

They exchanged numbers, and Libbie tried to remain composed, despite the excitement building inside her. Three respectable jobs with members of the community. She'd have enough money to make it through the summer.

Even better, she was one step closer to catering Mrs. Quincy's party of the season.

## FIFTEEN

Incredibly enough, Libbie received a text from her mom letting her know they were moving their barbecue to Sunday to accommodate Libbie's schedule. It was Nick's weekend, but he agreed to drop the kids off early. They worked most of the weekend anyway, and Nick and Courtney spent most of that time at Cone Hut together.

Libbie barely made it past the front door before her mother started. "I knew that guy was no good," her mother said. "It's those long eyelashes. I've always said you can't trust a man with feminine eyelashes."

"Mom," Libbie said in her warning tone. Thankfully, Josh and Courtney had already made their way through the house to find their cousins.

"What? You're trying to tell me he doesn't have long eyelashes?"

Libbie didn't want to debate 'feminine' eyelashes and their impact on someone's integrity. "I don't think we need to rip him apart. That's all." As angry and upset as Libbie was, having her family weigh in on the subject served no purpose other than to fan the flames.

Her mother walked beside her to join the others. "It's not as though your children put him up on a pedestal. They recognized trash better than their mother did."

"Still, he was a member of our family for the past three years, and he's the gym teacher at Josh's school. They're bound to have mixed feelings." Chris hadn't been all bad. If he had been, he wouldn't have lasted three years. He'd helped with ferrying the kids to and from swim lessons and other activities. He was there when they thought Josh had broken his arm and Nick wasn't home. It turned out to be a sprain, but Chris had taken control of the situation and kept his cool when talking to the hospital staff. Libbie had been too anxious to speak, let alone ask the necessary questions. He'd taken care of the bills, although Libbie knew she couldn't give him much credit for that under the circumstances.

"It was a mistake to let him move in when you weren't married," her father said, picking up the baton and carrying on.

Libbie glanced over at the kitchen table where her father sat in judgment.

"I'm glad I didn't marry him," Libbie said. It would've been a lot harder to untangle their intertwined lives if she'd made it official.

"I don't know why you can't find a decent man like your sister did," her father said. "It's not like you're damaged goods."

Libbie bristled. "I'm not 'goods' of any kind."

Her mother examined her closely. "You're very combative today. What's gotten into you?"

Defending herself from criticism was combative? The inner workings of her mother's mind never ceased to amaze her.

"Mom, can we play corn hole?" Josh asked, appearing in the family room. She had no doubt that her son had overheard the conversation and was making an effort to rescue her. It both impressed her and pained her. He was still a kid. He shouldn't have to worry about saving his mother from uncomfortable situations, especially from members of their own family.

"You should ask Emily," her father said. "She has a better arm."

"It's not the World Series, Pop-Pop," Josh said. "It's corn hole."

Libbie coughed to smother a laugh. "I'd love to play, honey. I'll be right there."

Josh cut through the living room to the patio door, and Ryan rushed after him. "I want to play," the younger boy said. Despite having an older brother of his own, Ryan seemed enamored of his cousin.

Josh waited for him at the back door. "You can be on my team."

Ryan looked ready to burst from delight. Libbie was heartened to see how well the cousins got along, despite her parents' efforts to pit them against each other. She hoped they never succumbed to the manufactured rivalry.

"What about you, Court?" Libbie asked.

Her daughter glanced up from her place on the couch where her nose was buried in her phone. "Can I finish this first?"

"Sure," Libbie said.

"You let them spend too much time on devices," her mother complained.

"She's drawing," Libbie said. "It's not like she's playing hours of video games."

"How can she be drawing? It's a phone."

Courtney held up the phone and showed them the screen. "It's a drawing app. I use my finger."

"That's not drawing," her father scoffed. "That's tracing."

To her credit, Courtney simply smiled. "I'm not tracing anything, Pop-Pop. I layer in files. Come and see."

Her father's brow furrowed. "That's okay. I don't need to see it."

"Emily's boys are outside all the time," her mother said. "Fresh air and exercise, that's what's important." She gave Courtney a pointed look. "If you want to stay thin, you'll spend less time in an ice cream shop and on your phone, and more time doing physical activities like your cousins."

Libbie's cheek began to pulse. "Please don't give my daughter body image issues. She's only thirteen." She marched to the patio door and realized that Courtney was behind her.

"I'll play, too," she said quietly, and Libbie knew her daughter didn't want to be left alone with her grandparents and endure another round of criticism. Smart girl.

Emily was outside setting up the game. She divided the bean bags and moved to the side. "Are you playing?"

"Let the kids go first since all four of them are out here."

The sisters stood together and spoke softly while the kids played. "Thanks for rearranging the day," Libbie said. The change had Emily's fingerprints all over it.

"A family get-together means all of us," Emily said. "Besides, the boys don't like it when it's just them."

"Can't say I blame them."

"I'm sorry about Chris. Let me know if you need any financial help."

"I'm fine," Libbie said quickly. She didn't want to give her family another reason to draw comparisons and put Libbie in a negative light.

"If it's any consolation, I never thought he'd do anything like that. If anything, I expected him to cheat."

Libbie stiffened. "Gee, thanks." She was beginning to regret sharing the truth with her family. She figured they'd hear about it through a third party eventually, though, and that would make it worse.

Emily grew flustered. "Sorry, I didn't mean it like that."

"It's fine," Libbie said. She was always the first to try to smooth things over. It was easier that way, although she was starting to recognize when to let things slide and when to take a stand.

"What are you going to do about the money? Do you think he'll pay you back?"

Libbie laughed. "Uh, no. I very much doubt it."

"Do you have any idea what he spent it on?" she asked.

She shook her head. "It doesn't matter. I'm looking forward, not back."

Emily eyed her with interest. "You sound pretty good, Lib. I thought you might not even come today. That maybe you'd cancel at the last minute and feign bad allergies."

Libbie was definitely guilty of that move in the past. "I feel pretty good, Em, all things considered. I'm excited about my catering business, and it's nice to have complete control of the remote."

Emily licked her lips, seemingly distrustful of her sister's response. "Aren't you scared? I mean, wouldn't it be better to just get a job?"

"Now you sound like Mom and Dad."

Emily ducked her head slightly. "God, you're right. I'm sorry. Well, I'll certainly pass your name along to anyone I know in need of a caterer."

"Thanks. I appreciate it."

They watched their kids finish a round of corn hole, and Libbie found herself enjoying the moment. She was thrilled that her parents had opted not to cook burgers and hot dogs today, so Libbie didn't worry about being sequestered at the grill.

They ate outside at the round table, and Libbie was grateful for the huge umbrella to protect herself from the sun. It was hot and humid today, and her clothes had begun to stick to her skin.

After dinner, Ryan begged for a round of the card game Uno, so Libbie and Emily cleared away the paper plates to make room. While in the kitchen, Libbie retrieved the tray she'd placed in the refrigerator upon arrival.

"From what I hear, Elizabeth, you've been spending time with everyone in town lately." Libbie's mother didn't bother to glance up from her Uno cards.

"I've been working," Libbie said. "They're not social calls." She held up a tray of food. "I brought a few mini-desserts I've been practicing. I'd like your feedback, if you don't mind." She placed the tray on the table and removed the lid.

"So you've brought us scraps?" her mother asked, wrinkling her nose.

Libbie frowned. "No. They're perfectly good. Think of them as tasters."

Emily leaned over to inspect the offerings. "I'll dig in."

"Me, too," Ryan said.

"Has Mrs. Quincy hired you for her Labor Day party yet?" her father asked.

"Not yet, but I'm getting closer to that possibility."

He looked at her skeptically. "That's a big deal. Are you sure you can handle it?"

Libbie bit her tongue, resisting the urge to offer a snarky reply. No good would come from it. "Yes, Dad. I'm positive I can handle it."

"You don't want to screw up a job like that," he continued. He placed a green '7' on the top of the pile. "You'll torpedo your business before it even gets off the ground."

"What makes you think I'll screw it up?" she asked. "I've held down a regular job for years. I'm raising two wonderful kids."

"You don't have a job now, do you?" her father pressed.

"Or a relationship," her mother added.

Libbie wanted to scream and hurl the tray of desserts at them. Instead, she kept her calm and said, "I do a damn good job, and I'm proud of what I've accomplished."

Her mother cut her a sideways glance. "Well, someone's been listening to her friend's self-help videos. This is Kate's influence."

"No, Mom. This is me."

Emily smiled at her sister. "I think what you're doing is great, and Mrs. Quincy will be lucky to hire you."

"Thanks, Em." Libbie warmed inside, grateful for her sister's support. So often it seemed their parents pitted them against each other. It was nice to know the wedge wasn't as wide as she feared.

Her mother tossed another card on the pile. "Do you think you'll have any sway with the guest list?"

Libbie balked. "Excuse me?"

Her mother spared her a glance. "I've always wanted to go to one of her parties. They're supposed to be fabulous."

"Mom, I'd be the caterer. I won't have any say over the guest list. Besides, you always host your own Labor Day party."

"I'll be there if she gets the job," Courtney said. "I'm going to help out."

Her mother's brow shot up. "You'd make your children wait on people we know?"

"She waits on people at Cone Hut," Libbie pointed out.

"Yes, I know." Libbie could tell from her mother's tone that she found that distasteful as well.

"I want to do it," Courtney said. "Mom's paying me, plus I want to help."

"I'm helping, too," Josh said. "I already asked my boss not to put me on the Labor Day schedule, just in case."

Libbie wanted to kiss her children. Truthfully, they hadn't discussed the Labor Day party, but just knowing that her kids would throw their weight behind her heartened her.

"If you need extra adult hands, I could help," Emily offered.

Libbie gaped at her sister. "Seriously? You'd do that?"

"Of course. The rest of the family could come here, and I'd go with you. Act as your sous chef or server. Whatever you need."

Given the size of Mrs. Quincy's party, there was a distinct possibility she'd need to take Emily up on her offer. "Thank you. That means a lot."

"Well, I hope you don't get the job in that case, or my own party will be ruined," her mother said.

Libbie ignored her. They played another round of Uno, followed by another round of corn hole before calling it a night.

By the time they left the house, Libbie felt drained. Her parents had a way of exhausting her store of emotional energy.

"I'm sorry they suck," Josh said.

Once in the car, Libbie turned to smile at her son. "But you don't, and that's all I care about."

"I love you, Mom," Courtney said from her place in the backseat.

"I love you, too, sweetheart."

Libbie dragged herself into the house and let out the dog, while Courtney attended to Eliza. Libbie decided to spend the remainder of the evening leafing through the books she'd ordered and try to learn more about her witchy abilities.

The kids disappeared upstairs, and Libbie settled on the couch with the books. She wanted to research the ingredients she'd used so far and see what the 'magic' books had to say about them. She was surprised when she opened Inga's book to find the first page missing, the one with the recipe for her own cocktail. Her fingers ran along the crease and she felt the jagged edges where the page had been torn.

She texted the kids, knowing each of them probably had a phone in hand right now.

> Did one of you rip out a page in the book Inga left to me? The one with the cocktail recipes.

> No, I haven't touched it.

Courtney was the first to respond, quickly followed by Josh.

Libbie stared at the book. Maybe it was part of the magic. Once the recipe was no longer needed, it disappeared, although that didn't explain the perforation.

Libbie set the book aside and started flipping through the pages of the other books. They provided in-depth information on the mythology behind the plants and the powers associated with them. *Aster amellus* was meant to drive away serpents. Begonias had the potential to grant psychic ability, but they were poisonous, so not recommended. The book then offered non-poisonous alternatives. Libbie found the information fascinating and didn't want to stop reading, even when her number of yawns increased and her eyes began to burn.

That night, she dreamed of dancing plants that reminded her of the cavorting broomsticks from the Mickey Mouse movie Fantasia. Acacia. Adonis. Aster. Zinnia. Potentilla. They bloomed in a variety of brilliant colors, and Libbie felt more connected to the earth than if she'd been physically sitting in the garden. It occurred to her, somewhere in the deep recesses of her mind, that the Mickey Mouse scene was about a sorcerer's apprentice. The comparison seemed apt. Except she was nobody's apprentice.

She was Elizabeth Stark, and she was her own witch.

# SIXTEEN

The day of Ethan's party, Libbie was as excited as if the party were her own. She'd been trying not to think about him, especially in light of the fact that she'd turned down his offer for dinner. She hoped she could get through the party with her resolve intact, but she knew it wouldn't be easy. Ethan Townsend was more tempting than her crab puffs.

He greeted her at the door, looking incredibly handsome in casual blue shorts and a hot pink Polo shirt. "Punctual as always."

"Can't let down my boss. He's got a real temper if you displease him," she teased. Of course, Ethan seemed like the most laidback guy in the world. It was hard to believe he was a lawyer.

He stood aside to let her pass. "You know where you're going. Do you need help unloading the car?"

"I can take care of it, thanks." She had two friends of Josh's working with her today as servers, but they weren't due to arrive until right before the guests.

"I don't mind." He held up his hands. "Idle hands and all that."

"You're about to throw a party for your clients. You shouldn't be idle. Go fluff your pillows or something."

He laughed. "They've been fluffed. The bar is ready. The view is viewable." He shrugged. "You're all I need now."

Libbie's throat tightened at his words. She knew he didn't mean them the way they sounded, but still. She made her way into the kitchen and kept her business hat on the whole time. This job was important to her. Serena had already reported her feedback to Mrs. Quincy, so she knew that was one five-star review under her belt. She needed this to go well. She couldn't allow her attraction to Ethan to distract her.

To his credit, he left her alone once the guests arrived. As she worked, she stole glances at him, noting how he interacted with his clients and their spouses. He was a natural with people. Smiling, laughing, shaking hands. Libbie felt her resistance fading the longer she watched him. He radiated positive energy and Libbie wanted to stand close to him and absorb it.

Aside from a minor mishap with a dish of bacon burger bites, the event ran smoothly. Libbie was relieved when the final guest made his exit. This particular client seemed in danger of sleeping on the sofa if he didn't leave soon. It was late, and Libbie had long since sent the servers home.

Ethan found her in the kitchen packing up. "Wow. What an amazing job you did. I can't thank you enough."

"No, thank you. I really needed this job, and I appreciate you taking a chance on me."

He leaned on the island and grinned at her. "No risk. No reward."

His words resonated with Libbie. Hadn't she found that to be true as well?

"Before I forget, I made something for you." She produced a small jar from her cooler.

He admired the gift. "What is it?"

"A cocktail. You pour it over ice, and it's ready. You might want to drink it another night, though. I think you've probably had your fill of booze tonight."

"You're not wrong." He scrutinized the contents. "Is it... witchy?"

Libbie couldn't resist a proud smile. "I infused it with amaranthus, which protects against cooking burns and household accidents."

He chuckled. "What are you trying to say? I'm a klutz?"

"Not at all, but I noticed the last time I was here that you had a burn mark from the oven on the side of your wrist. I created a recipe that should provide a little protection in the kitchen. It's the least I can do after all you've done for me."

He reached for the jar, his fingers brushing against hers, and Libbie felt a jolt of energy shoot through her.

"Now this doesn't mean I can take a flamethrower to the oven and nothing will happen, right?"

"Please, don't do that."

His hand closed over hers as he removed the jar from her grasp. "Thank you, Libbie."

With their eyes locked and the memory of his touch fresh in her mind, her whole body felt electrified. Still, she refused to give in to temptation. Technically, she was on the clock as his caterer. Kissing him right now would not be a good idea.

"Good night, Ethan. Thank you again." It took all her self-control to walk out the door without throwing herself into his arms, but she did it. She arrived home and took a cool shower before crawling into bed and succumbing to a long night of scandalous dreams.

Summer wore on, and the days seemed to run into each other. Libbie spent as much time learning about the magical properties of plants as she did perfecting recipes for her catering business. Instead of feeling tired and anxious, she was energized and optimistic. She'd received a few more inquiries and had booked a fiftieth birthday party for mid-September. It wouldn't yield the benefits of Mrs. Quincy's Labor Day party, but any event was good news as far as Libbie was concerned.

Frankie Smith hadn't been able to meet with her until close to the date of the party, so Libbie found herself scrambling afterward to get everything organized in time.

Frankie's home had a private lakeside beach, and that was where most of the party would be held. It meant that Libbie would spend most of the event on her own, which was generally the way she liked it.

As she prepped in the kitchen, Frankie walked in holding a silver wig in her hand, and Libbie was surprised to see that the hair on Frankie's head was so thin it was nearly transparent. She must've noticed Libbie's reaction because she immediately apologized. "I wasn't thinking. I can put it back on."

"Don't do that on my account," Libbie said. "I just wasn't expecting it."

"It's not really a secret, but I don't shout it from the rooftops either." She sighed. "A sign of aging, I'm afraid. My hair started to thin when I hit my forties, and it got worse each year, to the point that a wig became the only option. I chose silver to stay somewhat authentic."

"The wig looks amazing," Libbie said. "I never would've known if you hadn't taken it off."

"Thank you. That's kind of you to say." She stroked the hair on the wig. "Considering it costs about seven hundred dollars, it better look authentic." She smiled at Libbie. "But I suppose it's the price we pay to retain our youthful beauty. Unfortunately, it's not the only price. Botox, fillers, lashes." She gave a rueful shake of her head. "I wish I could say I didn't give a hoot, but I do. When I say I want to age gracefully, what I really mean is youthfully."

Libbie understood. Despite her growing confidence, she wasn't sure she'd want to rock a balding look either. That took a special type of confidence. Libbie hadn't quite reached that level yet, and hoped she never had to.

"And here I thought chronic fatigue and forgetfulness would be my menopause crosses to bear. If only I'd known." Frankie shrugged. "I suppose it wouldn't have made any difference. There's nothing you can do for thinning hair. If there were, men would have already solved that problem. There'd be Viagra for hair loss available in vending machines all over the world." She laughed at her own joke.

Libbie reached into her tote bag and pulled out her cocktail book. If recent events were any indication, there could very well be a cocktail recipe waiting for her.

"Ooh, is that the life-changing cocktail that Serena mentioned?" Frankie asked.

"It's a book of recipes I've been slowly making," she said. Looking through the book again, she was reminded of the missing page. The other recipes were still present and accounted for, so she wasn't sure what to think of it.

She turned to the most recent entry and then flipped past it. Sure enough, a new recipe was there—the ink sparkling with promise. "I think I might have one for you." She smiled at Frankie. "How do you feel about gin?"

"I'm a fan."

"Good. I'm about ready here, so I have time to prepare the infusion for your cocktail."

"That sounds intense."

To Libbie's relief, this recipe didn't require any overnight chilling in the refrigerator. "It's hand-crafted and can be easily ruined if you make a wrong move."

"Well, we wouldn't want that." She peered over the counter at Libbie's dishes. "I like everything I see. I wish it would've been feasible to have it all."

"Next time have a bigger budget," Libbie said with a smile.

"I think I've gained ten pounds just looking. I'll need to control myself today."

Libbie set to work making the cocktail and was pleased that she'd brought leek with her for one of the appetizers. It was as though the book *knew* what she'd have available.

"Leek in a cocktail?" Frankie queried. "How interesting."

Libbie remembered from one of the books that wild leek was connected to protection, love, and a lingering presence, among other things. She wondered which one would be active in the cocktail.

By the time Frankie's drink was in hand, her wig was back on, and the arrival of her guests had begun. Libbie had made Greek salad skewers and melon prosciutto skewers, along with pickle sushi, BLT cups, and a myriad of other handheld foods. Frankie had requested a menu heavy on finger foods, items that could be held in one hand and eaten. It was a fun challenge, and Libbie was pleased with the results.

She was in the middle of cleanup when a familiar figure appeared beside her. "Hildie?"

"Libbie, I'm so glad to see you." Hildie embraced her. "I heard you were catering, but every time I tried to make my way up here from the beach, someone intercepted me."

"That's okay. It's a party. You don't need to consort with the help. How is everything?"

"I have good news, and I have bad news," Hildie said. "Which would you like first?"

"Whatever order you want to tell me."

Hildie sucked in a breath. "The bad news is that I have breast cancer. Stage one."

Libbie's heart skipped a beat. She wasn't sure whether to congratulate her or commiserate. "Oh, Hildie."

"The good news is that we've caught it early, and the doctor said, as far as breast cancer goes, I couldn't have a better prognosis. I won't even need radiation."

"Wow, are you serious?"

"I will need a mastectomy, but you know, I always sort of had that knowledge in the back of my mind. And, to be honest, my boobs having been looking sad these last couple of years. It'll be nice to upgrade. Anyway, if I have to have cancer, it's the best-case scenario. Thanks to you, I worked up the courage to make the appointment."

Libbie knew what the end result of waiting would've been. "I'm glad you caught it early. Please let me know if you need help with anything after your surgery. I can even make meals for you and the family when you're not able to cook."

"Oh, Libbie. I'm not able to cook now." Hildie laughed. "Breast cancer has nothing to do with it."

"I mean, I'm glad it's a good prognosis, but, obviously, I wish you didn't have to go through this at all."

"Me, neither, but you were right. Ignoring it wouldn't make it go away. It would've just made it worse."

"When's the surgery?"

"Next week after the kids are back in school, so light a candle for me." .

"Of course I will." And if she could do more, she would.

"Well, I don't want to interrupt you while you're working, but I've been dying to tell you in person—that I'm not dying."

"I'm so glad, Hildie. Thank you." She watched her friend leave the house to rejoin the party and felt a tightening in her chest. She took a moment to thank her lucky stars that she was healthy and relatively happy—and growing happier by the day.

Libbie was bone-tired by the end of the party, but it was the good kind where she knew she'd worked hard and felt good about what she'd accomplished. Frankie had been thrilled with the outcome, and Libbie had spotted her dancing wigless on the beach amidst the lit torches.

As she dropped into the driver's seat of her car, her phone buzzed with a call from Kate. "Hey, there," Libbie said. "I just finished Frankie Smith's party. What's up?"

"Did it go well?"

"I think so." And, if so, it was lucky number three. Frankie had promised to send a good word to Mrs. Quincy first thing tomorrow.

"Good," Kate said. "I'm glad you had one positive today because I'm about to drop a negative in your lap. Apologies in advance."

Libbie stiffened behind the wheel. "What's wrong?"

"G.G. is in the hospital." G.G. stood for Gerti Gatti, the princi-pal's secretary at the high school. Everyone in town knew the cheerful older woman. She seemed to show up at every community event that involved the local kids. Despite her arthritis and bad hip, she was their biggest cheerleader.

"That's a shame. What from?"

"She's sick from a poison she ingested. From what I understand, she said that she drank a cocktail Chris had given her, promising that it would help her arthritis. The bastard even charged her for it."

Libbie's body grew cold as she remembered the missing page in the book. She'd never changed the locks at the house. She hadn't thought it was necessary.

"Libbie? Did you hear me?"

"Yes." Her response was muted but audible. "Is she going to be okay?"

"It's unclear. She's on a ventilator, and the police are looking for Chris. If there's any chance he'll come to hide in your house, you might want to get home."

The pressure of tears built behind Libbie's eyes as she pictured poor G.G., sick and helpless in a hospital bed. Instinctively she wanted to blame herself. No, she thought, stopping that guilt train in its tracks. This wasn't her fault. This was Chris's doing, pure and simple. Once again, his greed and laziness had won out over common decency. Libbie felt nauseated by the thought of him.

She started the car and headed for home, silently praying with each passing mile that he wouldn't be there.

# SEVENTEEN

Libbie's palms were sticky with sweat as she pulled into the driveway. Although Chris's car wasn't visible from the road, she could see the rear of it sticking out from behind a cluster of trees on the side of the house. She was relieved the kids weren't home. What was his plan? Hide out here until the police grew bored searching for him?

She shook her head as she opened the front door, knowing perfectly well she'd find it unlocked. "Chris?" she called.

Hercules rushed to greet her, and she heard Eliza cry from the top of the stairs. She entered the kitchen with the dog by her side. Chris stood at the counter, cracking open a beer.

"Did you come to return the page you stole from me?" she asked, her voice as sharp as her chef's knife. She withdrew the book from her tote bag and set it on the counter.

He avoided her gaze. "I don't know what I did wrong. I only substituted the garnish thing because I didn't have any."

Libbie drew a steadying breath. "What did you replace it with?"

"Apparently, it's called poison parsley, but I didn't know. It was just some wild herb I found when I was hiking. That's how I got the idea. I didn't think it mattered what I used."

"Why would you do that?"

He glared at her. "What? You're the only one allowed to make money? You always wanted me to earn a summer income, so that's what I was trying to do."

"I don't sell cocktail recipes, Chris. I'm running a catering business. The cocktails are for friends for fun." A necessary lie. "And why would you tell her it would help her arthritis anyway? You have to know that's not true."

He shrugged. "I thought the alcohol would loosen her up, and she wouldn't ache so much from her joints."

He really was an idiot.

Chris opened the book with idle fingers and froze. "Wait. How did it get back in here?" He flipped back and forth between pages. "Did you recreate it?"

"What are you talking about?" Libbie asked.

He gripped a page in the book. "This is the recipe I tore out. The one I used for G.G."

Libbie peered at him. "I'm sure it isn't."

"It definitely is." He met her gaze. "What the hell, Libbie?"

She recognized the stubborn look in his eye. She was never going to get rid of him unless she took a stand now. Even if she called the police, it would be a temporary measure. He'd keep coming by when she least expected it to harass her and belittle her. Libbie squared her shoulders.

No more.

"I'm sure it's a different one. How about I make it for you and prove it?"

Chris frowned. "You want to make me a drink?"

"Sure," she said, smiling sweetly. "Why not? A toast to our separate ways, and no hard feelings. Much nicer than that cheap beer you're drinking."

His mouth twisted into a wolfish grin. "I'm not one to turn down booze."

"Why would you?" Libbie smiled over her shoulder as she shifted the book to the opposite counter where the liquor cabinet was located. She swayed her hips provocatively, knowing it would draw his gaze, and opened the other book that lay nearby, the one she'd been reading about magical plants. She bit down on her lip and hoped he didn't notice the change in focus.

She mixed the cocktail as quickly as she could, grateful that she'd spotted the necessary ingredient beforehand. She'd actually had the thought when she'd seen it, but had brushed it aside, thinking she was overreacting. She knew now that she hadn't been. There'd be no second chance.

"I just need an ingredient from the garden," she said. She hurried past him with Hercules hot on her heels. She raced to the garden and pinched what she needed before returning to the kitchen.

Libbie remained calm as her hands worked on autopilot. She lifted the shaker and pretended it was a maraca, smiling the whole time.

"You've gotten pretty good at this," he said. "You should consider picking up shifts at one of the lakeshore bars if you need money."

*If you need money.*

Libbie wanted to haul off and punch him in the throat. Keeping her cool, she poured the contents of the shaker into a glass and added the final touch—the most important part of the spell. She handed him the glass with a sultry smile.

"Bottoms up."

He leered at her. "If you're lucky."

Inwardly, she cringed. How had she ever found him attractive? It was as though she saw him clearly for the first time. He'd never touch her again. Not even a handshake.

He downed the drink in two gulps. In typical Chris fashion, he didn't bother to savor the carefully crafted flavors. She leaned a hip against the counter, waiting. His sour expression told her the moment the spell began to take effect.

"What's in this?" He glared at her.

"Alcohol, Chris. That's why it's called a cocktail."

He advanced toward her. "It burns. Why does it burn?" He clutched his chest and started to choke.

Libbie remained rooted in place. "Because it's a banishing spell, Chris. It's the same one I'd use to repel cockroaches." She folded her arms, satisfied. "And now it's banishing you. Appropriate, don't you think?"

"What the hell are you talking about? You sound like a lunatic." Then his whole body stiffened, seemingly against his will.

"You've been cast out of this house, Chris, never to return. Good luck finding a lawyer. I might not have been willing to sue you, but poisoning an old lady is a whole different story."

And she knew one lawyer who wouldn't represent him.

In one final move of defiance, Chris lunged for the book and grabbed it as the spell took hold. He flew backward through the house with Libbie chasing after him.

"No," she cried as the front door opened on its own. He continued backward, like a puppet on a string, and straight outside. The door slammed shut between them, and her hands splayed on the glass. "Stop!"

He landed on his backside and rolled to his feet, still holding the book. "Didn't expect me to take this, huh? I bet you're nothing without this stupid book." His mouth twisted in a heinous smile as he slipped a free hand into his pocket and produced a lighter. So he was smoking again? Not the way she wanted to find out.

"Chris, don't," Libbie shouted, grabbing the door handle. Everything seemed to happen in slow motion. He flicked the lighter, and a small flame erupted. She raced outside and watched him set the book alight. In one deliberate motion, he dropped the burning book onto the ground and swaggered toward his car. Tears streamed down Libbie's face as she ran to the book. She kicked dirt over it, dousing the flames, and dropped to her knees beside it.

"No, no, *no.*" She could see the crisp black edges of the pages. What happened now? Was she still a witch? Would she lose her connection to Inga forever?

A police siren alerted her to their arrival. Chris didn't make it to his car. They arrested him right there in her driveway and she watched with a mixture of satisfaction and revulsion as they drove away with Chris in the backseat.

A Land Rover pulled into the driveway just as the police disappeared from view. Kate hopped out and ran to her side.

"Libbie, are you okay? I saw the cop car."

"The book," Libbie croaked.

Kate glanced at the ground where the book still rested. "That asshole! He burned Inga's book?"

Libbie tried to hold back the tears, but they pushed their way forward. A fat teardrop landed on the top page. She watched in amazement as the black edges faded, and the words reformed as though nothing had happened. She blinked away the remaining tears and lifted the book to study it. Every page was intact, even the one he'd torn out. Every recipe legible. And, even better, Chris wouldn't be able to set foot on her property ever again.

Kate gaped at the book. "Did you see that?"

"How could I miss it?"

"You just..." Kate was at a loss for words, not a common experience.

"I know. I just Rapunzeled the book." And she didn't even have a Sundrop flower.

What she did have, however, was magic.


The first call she received the next day was from Kate, and it was good news. G.G. was off the ventilator, and it appeared she would make a full recovery. Libbie sank against her pillow, relief flooding her body. She planned to meet Kate at the hospital later and pay G.G. a visit. It was the least she could do.

She'd made it downstairs to the coffee machine when the kids arrived home from their dad's. She wasn't even bothered that Josh had dark circles under his eyes from lack of sleep. Nick had never been great about enforcing bedtime.

"Did you hear about G.G.?" Josh asked.

"I did. It sounds like she's going to be okay."

"Olivia said Chris had something to do with it," Courtney said. Libbie sensed her daughter's anxiety kicking in.

"It was an accident, honey, but I can promise you that Chris won't be coming here anymore. I made sure of it, so there's no need to worry."

"I heard he's going to lose his job," Josh said. "The principal is furious."

"Even grownups can lose their way sometimes," Libbie said. "Hopefully, one day, he'll find his."

She'd just brought the steaming cup of coffee to her lips when the next call came through. Although it was a local exchange, Libbie didn't recognize the number. Normally she would let the call go to voicemail, but curiosity got the better of her.

"Hello?"

"Libbie Stark, this is Sylvia Quincy."

Libbie halted all movement, including her breath. "Good morning," she said, quickly recovering. "How are you?"

"Excellent. I want to let you know that I've heard nothing but amazing things about you. What's more, as long as you make those puffs everyone's raving about, you've got the job."

Libbie swallowed a cry of triumph. "Thank you so much, Mrs. Quincy. You won't regret it."

"Come by tomorrow at four to see the space, and we'll go over the menu." She gave Libbie the address, although everyone in Lake Cloverleaf knew where the Quincys lived.

"I'll be there. Thanks again."

"Good news?" Josh asked.

Libbie's smile was so wide that her cheeks ached. "Very good news. How would you two like to help me out on Labor Day?"

"You really want me to help?" Courtney asked. "I thought that was only to annoy Grandma."

"Of course I want your help. You've been working with your dad all summer. You're an expert employee by now."

Courtney glanced down at her feet. "Are you sure? What if I mess up? It sounds like this is a big deal."

Libbie crossed the room to kiss her daughter on the cheek. "You're a responsible young woman, and I trust you." Libbie could practically feel her daughter's elation.

"Do I get to wear a tux?" Courtney asked.

"I don't think so. It's still summer, so I imagine the theme will reflect that."

"If I have to wear a tux, I'm definitely working at the club that day." Josh bit a banana in half.

"I think your boss is willing to be flexible." It occurred to her that she could use more than two servers for a party as large as the Quincy's. "What would you think if I asked Caeden Kitts to help out?"

"It's not like he needs to work," Josh said.

"I know, but I get the sense his parents would like to see him a bit more active."

And she suspected this Labor Day party would have more than its share of artistic inspiration. The Quincy's house was legendary.

Josh shrugged. "Fine with me. Let me know if you need anyone else. I bet I can ask some friends from the club."

"Great, thanks."

Libbie's gaze drifted to Inga's book on the counter, fully intact. Two weeks ago, her life seemed to be falling apart at the seams, and now she wasn't sure if it could get much better. If this was the life of a witch, then it was time to fire up the cauldron because Libbie Stark was fully committed.

# EIGHTEEN

Mrs. Quincy treated her Labor Day party the way John Hammond treated Jurassic Park—she spared no expense. Although Libbie knew this would be *the* party of the season, she hadn't realized exactly how big of a job it would be until she started planning. Thankfully, Mrs. Quincy wasn't a difficult client. She seemed to delight in Libbie's ideas and was flexible when Libbie suggested alternatives to Mrs. Quincy's usual way of doing things.

In Libbie's eyes, the Quincy house was one of the most impressive in town. If she could choose any house in Lake Cloverleaf, it would be this traditional American style, with its light blue siding trimmed in white. A balcony overlooked the front lawn, and two more balconies wrapped around either side of the house to take advantage of the views.

"Wow," Courtney breathed.

Libbie smiled at her daughter. "I know, right?"

"You can have that wing when I live here." Courtney pointed to the left.

"Good, that side has the better view."

Mrs. Quincy greeted her at the door in a red and white print maxi dress and thonged feet. "There's my crew."

"Mrs. Quincy, I'd like you to meet two of my staff today. This is my son, Josh, and my daughter, Courtney. My sister Emily will be here shortly."

"A family affair," she said. "I like it. Come on in, dolls. I'm happy you're here."

They followed her through to the main kitchen and straight into the butler's kitchen. It was smaller than the main kitchen, but still equipped with nicer appliances than Libbie had in her own house. In fact, they were nicer than anything at Basecamp, too. Libbie had nearly salivated over them when she'd shown up to finalize the menu a few days earlier.

"This is great. Thank you." Libbie liked that she'd be able to work in the private kitchen because it cut down on distractions. She needed this party to go off without a hitch. It was one thing to land the job, but she also had to make it a rousing success.

"What's this book?" Mrs. Quincy asked, noticing the black leather-bound book Libbie had placed on the counter. She made a habit of traveling everywhere with it now, in case inspiration struck her.

"I've been working on recipes for some unique cocktails. I like to have the book with me in case I get an idea while I'm working. Sometimes the ingredients I use in cooking end up in a glass of tequila." She smiled. "I bet these would really wow your guests."

She arched an eyebrow. "Is that so? I do like to wow people. I consider it one of my signature moves." Her gaze flicked to the book. "I should probably let you stick to the script, but selfishly, I'd like to take one for a test drive."

"I can make you one later. I'll have time."

Mrs. Quincy nodded approvingly. "I admire your confidence, Libbie. I'll leave you to it then. Give me a shout if you need me." She sailed out of the room, and Libbie went straight to work, issuing instructions to the kids. Emily arrived not long after and Libbie welcomed her with a warm hug.

"I really appreciate you helping out," Libbie said.

"You're my sister. If you need my help, I'm here."

Emily took charge of instructing the kids on which trays to take out and when, and left Libbie to focus solely on the food. Halfway through the party, there was a slight bump when Emily reported there were no more crab puffs.

"Can you make more?" Emily asked. "People are raving about them."

"I could, except I'm out of crab." Libbie's stomach lurched at the prospect of improvising, but she quickly brushed her fears aside. She'd spent most of her adult life improvising when life threw her a curveball, both as a mother and a chef. Many times a Basecamp special had gone awry, and Libbie had solved the problem. There was no reason to panic now.

"We have cheese, don't we?" she asked.

Emily ran to the refrigerator and yanked open the door. "Gruyere and cheddar."

"Perfect. I need both." She knew she had everything she needed to make an alternative dish that would be just as well received. She barely noticed as the servers came and went; she was too intent on finishing the puffs and circulating them as quickly as possible.

The party was nearly over by the time she drew breath. It was a much bigger job than the others she'd catered, but she'd enjoyed every minute of it.

"Libbie, these puffs are heavenly." Mrs. Quincy sauntered into the butler's kitchen with a martini in one hand and a half-eaten puff in the other.

"Thank you." Libbie opted not to tell her about the crab crisis since no one had seemed to notice the switcheroo.

"All your choices are spot on, and they look as good as they taste." She popped the remaining puff in her mouth and sighed contentedly. "Better than sex. But don't tell my husband."

"My lips are sealed."

"My dear, I am so thrilled with everything you've done. I'll be spreading the word all over town and in my salons. You're going to be so busy between now and Christmas, you won't be able to spend all the money you're making."

"That's fine with me," Libbie said. "I have two kids heading to college." One sooner rather than later.

Mrs. Quincy glanced over her shoulder toward the main part of the house. "They're doing a wonderful job out there. So polite and well-spoken. You should be very proud. You're doing a lot right."

"Thank you. There's no higher compliment."

"I'll let you get back to work, but make sure you come out and mingle a little. Show your face to the guests. I'd be sure to introduce yourself to Holly Munson and Patrick Broderick." She lowered her voice to a whisper. "One throws an annual Christmas party, and the other does New Year's. Trust me, you want them as clients." She gestured with her fingers to indicate money.

"I appreciate the tip."

Mrs. Quincy raised her glass before twirling on her heel and exiting the kitchen.

Libbie took a moment to digest the exchange. Mrs. Quincy was thrilled and would be recommending her services.

The party was a success.

She tipped back her head and inhaled deeply. Everything was going to be okay. *She* was going to be okay.

Better than okay, really. And it was all because she'd taken a chance and blown up her seemingly comfortable life. She'd thought it was a mistake that she'd regret, and instead it was turning out to be the best thing that ever happened to her, outside of her children.

*How could I make that experience the best thing that ever happened to me?*

A lone tear escaped as she realized that she'd done exactly that. This was so much sweeter than lemons into lemonade.

"Mom, what's wrong?" Courtney entered the kitchen wearing a concerned expression.

Libbie fished a tissue from her pocket and wiped away the tears. "Nothing, sweetheart. Everything is exactly as it should be." She'd be able to pay the mortgage company, which meant she'd be able to keep a roof over their heads.

"Does this mean Mrs. Quincy is happy with you?"

Libbie enveloped her daughter in a tight embrace. "Mrs. Quincy is very happy with me. But, more importantly, *I* am very happy with me."

Courtney smiled up at her mother. "I'm happy with me, too."

Libbie felt a sense of relief. Just because she'd waited until she was forty-eight to lessen her anxiety didn't mean she wanted that for her daughter. She wanted Courtney to grow up feeling confident and loved and, thanks to Inga, she knew they were on the right track.

By the time Friday night rolled around, Libbie was excited to see her friends again and share all that had happened during the week. It seemed like months had passed since their last cocktail club meeting. She'd been so busy that she hadn't even had a chance to catch up with them over text messages.

Tonight, they met at Libbie's house because the kids and Hercules were with Nick. Only Eliza lurked in the background, emerging from the shadows once the other women arrived.

"You've come to say hello, have you?" Rebecca crouched down to address the cat.

Eliza meowed and rubbed against her.

"She probably smells her sisters," Libbie said.

"How are she and Hercules getting along?" Rebecca asked.

"Great, actually. She cries when he's away for the weekend. Who would've suspected?"

Rebecca stroked the cat's soft fur. "She'll get plenty of attention tonight. Auntie Rebecca's here to hang out with you. Yes, she is."

"I thought you were here to hang out with us," Kate said.

Rebecca resumed a standing position. "Can't it be both?"

Libbie motioned to the table. "I have plenty of snacks, so I hope you're hungry."

"Screw the snacks," Kate said. "Where are the cocktails?"

"Patience, grasshopper," Libbie said. "I'm mixing something special."

Julie grimaced. "You and your special cocktails. What about us? Why haven't we gotten our magic?"

"You have it," Libbie assured her. "It just hasn't manifested yet. At least that's Lorraine's take."

Kate gave her a prim look. "I'm sure mine will kick in soon."

From her place at the kitchen counter, Libbie gave her friend a sympathetic smile. "I'm sure it will, too."

"I don't care if nothing changes for me," Rebecca said. "Watching Libbie punch her way out of the cocoon has been glorious."

"Here, here," Kate said. "Get over here, Madame Butterfly. We want you present and accounted for."

"Give me one second. I just got a voicemail." Libbie's insides twisted at the sight of Ethan's name on her screen.

"I bet it's Silver Fabio," Julie said. "I can tell from that grin on her face."

Libbie ignored them as she went into the other room to listen to his message.

"Hi, Libbie. I'm respecting your space, but I wanted to let you know that I've reached out to both of my biological parents. I haven't heard back yet, but, you know, that first step was the doozy. Anyway, that never would've happened if not for you, so thank you. I owe you one."

Libbie sighed into the phone. The mere thought of Ethan took her breath away.

"Just go out with him, would you?" Kate hovered in the doorway. "What are you afraid of?"

Libbie met her friend's gaze. "Nothing. Nothing at all." She pulled up "Ethan" and sent a quick text.

I'd like to take you up on your offer of dinner, if you're still interested.

The reply was swift and immediate.

Always interested in a woman who texts with full spelling and punctuation. Tomorrow night—dinner at my house?

Libbie smiled to herself and replied.

I'll ride over on my broomstick.

"Someone looks pleased," Julie said, as Libbie and Kate reentered the room. "Spill it, sister."

Libbie tucked away the phone. "I will when there's something to spill."

"Just don't spill the tequila," Rebecca said.

Libbie resumed her place at the counter and eyed the recipe in her book.

"What are you mixing?" Kate asked.

Libbie shooed her friend away. "A witch never reveals her secrets."

Julie perked up. "One for each of us?"

"Yes." Libbie smiled as she prepared the zinnia-infused cocktail. She filled four glasses and made a sweeping gesture. "A Libbie Stark creation. I've named it The Inga."

"What are you up to, Lib? Is this for hot flashes or something?" Rebecca asked.

"No, this one is for remembering an absent friend." Libbie brought two glasses over, followed by the second pair.

"I know how we can remember an absent friend," Kate said. "Why don't we do a compliment circle?"

"Yes, let's do one for Inga," Julie agreed.

Libbie thought that was a wonderful idea. She sipped the cocktail and savored the balance of sweet and sour. "I'll start. Inga was —and still is—an inspiration to me."

"And you're quickly following in her footsteps," Kate added.

Libbie nudged her with an elbow. "This is Inga's compliment circle," she whispered.

"May my final witch form be as impressive as Inga's," Kate said.

"What makes you think this isn't your final witch form?" Libbie asked.

"Because my book is as blank as Lucas's face when I ask him where the remote is," Kate said.

Libbie stifled a laugh.

"Whenever I think of Inga, I feel lighter. Happier." Julie punctuated her compliment with a smile.

"Inga sparkled," Rebecca said. "I think that *Twilight* lady got it all wrong. Vampires don't sparkle. Witches do."

Libbie glanced down at herself. "I don't know. Am I sparkling?"

"Yes," the others replied in unison.

Libbie laughed and raised her glass. "To Inga," Libbie said.

"To Inga," the others repeated. They raised their glasses to join hers and clinked.


The next morning a happily hungover Libbie sat at the kitchen table with the laptop and logged into her bank account.

"What are you doing, Mom?" Courtney asked.

She smiled at her daughter. "Paying the bills." It felt freeing to say those words out loud.

Courtney joined her at the table. "Why do you sound so happy about it?"

She typed in the full amount that she owed the mortgage company and clicked the button with a satisfied sigh. "Because it's a good feeling to be able to take care of yourself."

"That makes sense." Courtney paused and scrunched her nose. "Will you still live in my mansion when you're old?"

Libbie laughed. "I think I'd prefer to let you live your own life in peace. I'll do my best to make sure I have the means to take care of myself."

There would be plenty of time for that. Middle age wasn't the end of the road.

For Libbie, it was only the beginning.

# A LETTER FROM THE AUTHOR

Huge thanks for reading *Magic Uncorked*. I hope you were hooked on Libbie's journey. If you want to join other readers in hearing all about my new releases and bonus content, you can sign up for my newsletter!

www.stormpublishing.co/annabel-chase

If you enjoyed this book and could spare a few moments to leave a review that would be hugely appreciated. Even a short review can make all the difference in encouraging a reader to discover my books for the first time. Thank you so much!

Thanks again for being part of this amazing journey with me and I hope you'll stay in touch – I have so many more stories and ideas to entertain you with!

Annabel Chase x

www.annabelchase.com

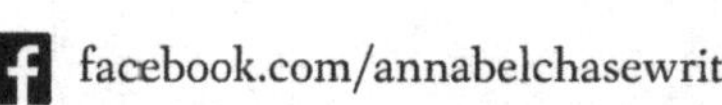

facebook.com/annabelchasewriter

x.com/AuthorAnnabel

instagram.com/annabelchaseauthor